THE HORROR
FROM THE HILLS

THE HORROR
FROM THE HILLS

Frank Belknap Long

WILDSIDE PRESS

THE HORROR FROM THE HILLS

1. The Coming of the Stone Beast

IN A LONG, low-ceilinged room adorned with Egyptian Graeco-Roman, Minoan and Assyrian antiquities a thin, careless-seeming young man of twenty-six sat jubilantly humming. As nothing in his appearance or manner suggested the scholar—he wore grey tweeds of Ivy League cut; a pin-striped blue shirt with a buttoned-down collar and a ridiculously brilliant necktie—the uninitiated were inclined to regard him as a mere supernumerary in his own office. Strangers entered unannounced and called him "young man" at least twenty times a week, and he was frequently asked to convey messages to a non-existent superior. No one suspected, no one dreamed until he enlightened them, that he was the lawful custodian of the objects about him; and even when he revealed his identity people surveyed him with distrust and were inclined to suspect that he was ironically joking with them.

· Algernon Harris was the young man's name and postgraduate degrees from Yale and Oxford set him distinctly

7

apart from the undistinguished majority. But it is to his credit that he never paraded his erudition, nor succumbed to the impulse—almost irresistible in a young man with academic affiliations—to put a Ph.D. on the title page of his first book.

It was this book which endeared him to the directors of the Manhattan Museum of Fine Arts and prompted their unanimous choice of him to succeed the late Halpin Chalmers as Curator of Archaeology when the latter retired in the fall of the previous year.

In less than six months young Harris had exhaustively familiarized himself with the duties and responsibilities of his office and was becoming the most successful curator that the museum had ever employed. So boyishly ebullient was he, so consumed with investigative zeal, that his field workers contracted his enthusiasm as though it were a kind of fever and sped from his presence to trust their scholarly and highly cultivated lives to the most primitive of native tribes in regions where an outsider was still looked upon with suspicion, and was always in danger of bringing down the thunder.

And now they were coming back—for days now they had been coming back—occasionally with haggard faces. and once or twice, unfortunately, with something radically wrong with them. The Symons tragedy was a case in point. Symons was a Chang Dynasty specialist, and he had been obliged to leave his left eye and a piece of his nose in a Buddhist temple near a place called Fen Chow Fu. But when Algernon questioned him he could only mumble something about a small malignant face with corpsy eyes that had glared and glared at him out of a purple mist. And Francis Hogarth lost eighty pounds and a perfectly

8

good right arm somewhere between Lake Rudolph and Naivasha into the Anglo Egyptian Sudan.

But a few inexplicable and hence, from a scientific point of view, unfortunate occurrences were more than compensated for by the archaeological treasures that the successful explorers brought back and figuratively dumped at Algernon's feet. There were mirrors of Graeco-Bactrian design and miniature tiger-dragons or too-tiehs from Central China dating from at least 200 B.C., enormous diorite Sphinxes from the Valley of the Nile, "Geometric" vases from Mycenaean Crete, incised pottery from Messina and Syracuse, linens and spindles from the Swiss Lakes, sculptured lintels from Yucatan and Mexico, Mayan and Manabi monoliths ten feet tall, Palaeolithic Venuses from the rock caverns of the Pyrenees, and even a series of rare bilingual tablets in Hamitic and Latin from the site of Carthage.

It is not surprising that so splendid a garnering should have elated Algernon immoderately and impelled him to behave like a college junior at a fraternity-house jamboree. He addressed the attendants by their first names, slapped them boisterously upon their shoulders whenever they had occasion to approach him, and went roaming haphazardly about the building immersed in ecstatic reveries. So far indeed did he descend from his pedestal that even the directors were disturbed, and it is doubtful if anything short of the arrival of Clark Ulman could have jolted him out of it.

Ulman may have been aware of this, for he telephoned first to break the news mercifully. He had apparently heard of the success of the other expeditions and hated infernally to intrude his skeleton at the banquet. Algernon, as

9

we have seen, was humming, and the jingling of a phone-bell at his elbow was the first intimation he had of Ulman's return. Hastily detaching the receiver he pressed it against his ear and injected a staccato "What is it?" into the mouthpiece.

There ensued a silence. Then Ulman's voice, disconcertingly shrill, forced him to hold the receiver a little further from his ear. "I've got the god, Algernon, and I'll be over with it directly. I've three men helping me. It's four feet high and as heavy as granite. Oh, it's a strange, loathsome thing, Algernon. An unholy thing. I shall insist that you destroy it! "

"What's that?" Algernon raised his voice incredulously.

"You may photograph it and study it, but you've got to destroy it. You'll understand when you see what—*what I have become*! "

There came a hoarse sobbing, while Algernon struggled to comprehend what the other was driving at.

"It has wreaked its malice on me—on me . . ."

With a frown Algernon re-cradled the receiver and began agitatedly to pace the room. "The elephant-god of Tsang! " he muttered to himself. "The horror Richardson drew before—before they impaled him. It's unbelievable. Ulman has crossed the desert plateau on foot—he's crossed above the graves of Steelbrath, Talman, McWilliams, Henley and Holmes. Richardson swore the cave was guarded night and day by hideous yellow abnormalities. I'm sure that's the phrase he used—abnormalities without faces—subhuman worshippers only vaguely man-like, in thrall to some malign wizardry. He averred they moved in circles about the idol on their hands and knees,

10

and participated in a rite so foul that he dared not describe it.

"His escape was a sheer miracle. He had displayed extraordinary courage and endurance when they had tortured him, and it was merely because they couldn't kill him that the priest was impressed. A man who can curse valiantly after three days of agonizing torture must of necessity be a great magician and wonder-worker. But it couldn't have happened twice. Ulman could never have achieved such a break. He is too frail—a day on their cross would have finished him. They would never have released him and decked him out with flowers and worshipped him as a sort of subsidiary elephant-god. Richardson predicted that no other white man would ever get into the cave alive. And as for getting out . . .

"I can't imagine how Ulman did it. If he encountered even a few of Richardson's beast-men it isn't surprising he broke down on the phone. 'Destroy the statue!' Imagine! Sheer insanity, that. Ulman is evidently in a highly nervous and excitable state and we shall have to handle him with gloves."

There came a knock at the door.

"I don't wish to be disturbed," shouted Algernon irritably.

"We've got a package for you, sir. The doorman said for us to bring it up here."

"Oh, all right. I'll sign for it."

The door swung wide and in walked three harshly-breathing shabbily dressed men staggering beneath a heavy burden.

"Put it down there," said Algernon, indicating a spot to the rear of his desk.

11

The men complied with a celerity that amazed him.

"Did Mr. Ulman send you?" he demanded curtly.

"Yes, sir." The spokesman's face had formed into a moulding of relief. "The poor guy said he'd be here himself in half an hour."

Algernon started. "What kind of talk is that?" he demanded. "He doesn't happen to be a 'guy' but I'll pretend you didn't say it. Why the 'poor'? That's what I'm curious about. "

The spokesman shuffled his feet. "It's on account of his face. There's something wrong with it. He keeps it covered and won't let nobody look at it." ·

"Good God! " murmured Algernon. "They've mutilated him! "

"What's that, sir? What did you say?"

Algernon collected himself with an effort. "Nothing. You may go now. The doorman will give you a dollar. I'll phone down and tell him."

Silently the men filed out. As soon as the door closed behind them Algernon strode into the centre of the room and began feverishly to strip the wrapping from the thing on the floor. He worked with manifest misgivings, the distaste in his eyes deepening to disgust and horror as the massive idol came into view.

Words could not adequately convey the repulsiveness of the thing. It was endowed with a trunk and great, uneven ears, and two enormous tusks protruded from the corners of its mouth. But it was not an elephant. Indeed, its resemblance to an actual elephant was, at best, sporadic and superficial, despite certain unmistakable points of similarity. The ears were *webbed and tentacled*, the trunk terminated in a huge flaring disk at least a foot in diameter, and the tusks, which intertwined and interlocked at the base of the statue, were as translucent as rock crystal.

The pedestal upon which it squatted was of black onyx: the statue itself, with the exception of the tusks, had apparently been chiselled from a single block of stone, and was so hideously mottled and eroded and discoloured that it looked, in spots, as thought it had been dipped in sanies.

The thing sat bolt upright. Its forelimbs were bent stiffly at the elbow, and its hands—it had human hands—rested palms upward on its lap. Its shoulders were broad and square and its breasts and enormous stomach sloped outward, cushioning the trunk. It was as quiescent as a Buddha, as enigmatical as a sphinx, and as malignantly poised as a gorgon or cockatrice. Algernon could not identify the stone out of which it had been hewn, and its greenish sheen disturbed and puzzled him.

For a moment he stood staring uncomfortably into its little malign eyes. Then he shivered, and taking down a woollen scarf from the coatrack in the corner he cloaked securely the features which repelled him.

Ulman arrived unannounced. He advanced unobtrusively into the room and laid a tremulous hand on Algernon's shoulder. "Well, Algernon, how are you?" he murmured. "I—I'm glad to get back. Just to see—an old friend—is a comfort. I thought—but, well it doesn't matter. I was going to ask—to ask if you knew a good physician, but perhaps —I—I . . ."

Startled, Algernon glanced backward over his shoulder and straight into the other's eyes. He saw only the eyes, for the rest of Ulman's face was muffled by a black silk scarf.

"Clark!" he exclaimed. "By God, but you gave me a start!"

Rising quickly, he sent his chair spinning against the wall and gripped his friend affectionately by the shoulders. "It's good to see you again, Clark," he said, with a warm cordiality in his voice. "It's good—why, what's the matter?"

Ulman had fallen upon his knees and was choking and gasping for breath.

"I should have warned you not to touch me," he moaned. "I can't stand—being touched."

"But why . . ."

"The wounds haven't healed," he sobbed. "*It* doesn't want them to heal. Every night it comes and lays—the disk on them. I can't stand being touched."

Algernon nodded sympathetically. "I can imagine what you've been through, Clark," he said. "You must take a vacation. I'll have a talk with the directors about you tomorrow. In view of what you've done for us I'm sure I can get you at least four months. You can go to Spain and finish your *Glimpses into Pre-History*. Palaeontological anthropology is a soothing science, Clark. You'll forget all about the perplexities of mere archaeological research when you start poking about among bones and artifacts that haven't been disturbed since the Pleistocene."

Ulman had gotten to his feet and was staring at the opposite wall.

"You think that I have become—irresponsible?"

A look of sadness crept into Algernon's eyes. "No, Clark. I think you're merely suffering from—from non-psychotic, very transitory visual hallucinations. An almost unbearable strain can sometimes produce hallucinations when one's

14

sanity is in no way impaired, and considering what you've been through . . ."

"What I've been through!" Ulman caught at the phrase. "Would it interest you to know precisely what they did to me?"

Algernon nodded, meeting the other's gaze steadily.

"Yes, Clark. I wish to hear everything."

"They said that I must accompany Chaugnar Faugn into the world."

"Chaugnar Faugn?"

"That is the name they worship *it* by. When I told them I had come from the United States they said that Great Chaugnar had *willed* that I should be his companion.

" 'It must be carried,' they explained, 'and it must be nursed. If it is nursed and carried safely beyond the rising sun it will possess the world. And then all things that are now in the world, all creatures and plants and stones will be devoured by Great Chaugnar. All things that are and have been will cease to be, and Great Chaugnar will fill all space with its Oneness. Even its Brothers it will devour, its Brothers who will come down from the mountains ravening for ecstasy when it calls to them.' They didn't use precisely that term, because 'ecstasy' is a very sophisticated word, peculiar to our language. But that's the closest I can come to it. In their own aberrant way they were the opposite of unsophisticated.

"I didn't protest when they explained this to me. It was precisely the kind of break I had been hoping for. I had studied Richardson's book, you see, and I had read enough between the lines to convince me that Chaugnar Faugn's devotees were growing a little weary of it. It isn't a very

15

pleasant deity to have around. It has some regrettable and very nasty habits."

A horror was taking shape in Ulman's eyes.

"You must excuse my levity. When one is tottering on the edge of an abyss it isn't always expedient to dispense with irony. Were I to become wholly serious for a moment, were I to let the—what I believe, what I know to be the truth behind all that I'm telling you coalesce into a definite construction in my mind I should go quite mad. Let us call them merely regrettable habits.

"I guessed, as I say, that the guardians of the cave were not very enthusiastic about retaining Chaugnar Faugn indefinitely. It made—depredations. The guardians would disappear in the night and leave their clothes behind them, and the clothes, upon examination, would yield something rather ghastly.

"But however much your savage may want to dispose of his god the thing isn't always feasible. It would be the height of folly to attempt to send an omnipotent deity on a long journey without adequate justification. An angered god can take vengeance even when he is on the opposite side of the world. And that is why most barbarians who find themselves saddled with a deity they fear and hate are obliged to put up with it indefinitely.

"The only thing that can help them is a legend—some oral or written legend that will enable them to send their ogre packing without ruffling its temper. The devotees had such a legend. At a certain time, which the prophecy left gratifyingly indefinite, Chaugnar Faugn was to be sent out into the world. It was to be sent out to possess the world to its everlasting glory, and it was also written that those who sent it forth should be forever immune from its anger.

16

"I knew of the existence of this legend, and when I read Richardson and discovered what a vile and unpleasant customer the god was I decided I'd risk a trip across the desert plateau of Tsang."

"You crossed on foot?" interrupted Algernon with undisguised admiration.

"There were no camels available," assented Ulman. "I made it on foot. On the fourth day my water ran short and I was obliged to open a vein in my arm. On the fifth day I began to see mirages—probably of a purely hallucinatory nature. On the seventh day"—he paused and stared hard at Algernon—"on the seventh day I consumed the excrements of wild dogs."

Algernon shuddered. "But you reached the cave?"

"I reached the cave. The—the faceless guardians whom Richardson described found me grovelling on the sands in delirium a half-mile to the west of their sanctuary. They restored me by heating a flint until it was white-hot and laying it on my chest. If the high priest hadn't interfered I should have shared Richardson's fate."

"Good God!"

"The high priest was called Chung Ga and he was devilishly considerate. He took me into the cave and introduced me to Chaugnar Faugn.

"You've Chaugnar there," Ulman pointed to the enshrouded form on the floor, "and you can imagine what the sight of it squatting on its haunches at the back of an evil-smelling, atrociously lighted cave would do to a man who had not eaten for three days.

"I began to say very queer things to Chung Ga. I confided to him that Great Chaugnar Faugn was not just a lifeless statue in a cave, but a great universal god filling

17

all space—that it had created the world in a single instant by merely expelling its breath, and that when eventually it decided to inhale, the world would disappear. 'It also made this cave,' I hastened to add, 'and you are its chosen prophet.'

"The priest stared at me curiously for several moments without speaking. Then he approached the god and prostrated himself before it. 'Chaugnar Faugn,' he intoned, 'the White Acolyte has confirmed that you are about to become a great universal god filling all space. He will carry you safely into the world, and nurse you until you have no further need of him. The prophecy of Mu Sang has been most gloriously fulfilled.'

"For several minutes he remained kneeling at the foot of the idol. Then he rose and approached me. 'You shall depart with Great Chaugnar tomorrow,' he said. 'You shall become Great Chaugnar's companion and nurse.'

"I felt a wave of gratitude for the man. Even in my befuddled state I was sensible that I had achieved a magnificent break. 'I will serve him gladly,' I murmured, 'if only I may have some food.'

"Chung Ga nodded. 'It is my wish that you eat heartily,' he said. 'If you are to nurse Great Chaugnar you must consume an infinite diversity of fruits. And the flesh of animals. Red blood—red blood is Chaugnar's staff. Without it my god would suffer tortures no man could endure. It is impossible for a man to know how great can be the suffering of a god.'

"He tapped a drum and immediately I was confronted with a wooden bowl filled to the brim with pomegranate juice.

18

" 'Drink heartily,' he urged. 'I have reason to suspect that Chaugnar Faugn will be ravenous tonight.'

"I was so famished that I scarcely gave a thought to what he was saying and for fifteen minutes I consumed without discrimination everything that was set before me —evil-smelling herbs, ewe's milk, eggs, peaches and the fresh blood of antelopes.

"The priest watched me in silence. At last when I could eat no more he went into a corner of the cave and returned with a straw mattress. 'You have supped most creditably,' he murmured, 'and I wish you pleasant dreams.'

"With that he withdrew, and I crawled gratefully upon the mat. My strength was wholly spent and the dangers I still must face, the loathsome proximity of Great Chaugnar and the possibility that the priest had been deliberately playing a part and would return to kill me, were swallowed up in a physical urgency that bordered on delirium. Relaxing upon the straw I shut my eyes, and fell almost instantly into a deep sleep.

"I awoke with a start and a strange impression that I was not alone in the cave. Even before I opened my eyes I knew that something unspeakably malign was crouching or squatting on the ground beside me. I could hear it breathing in the darkness and the stench of it strangled the breath in my throat.

"Slowly, very slowly, I endeavoured to rise. An unsurpassably ponderous weight descended upon my chest and hurled me to the ground. I stretched out my hand to disengage it and met with an iron resistance. A solid wall of something cold, slimy and implacable rose up in the darkness to thwart me.

"In an instant I was fully awake and calling frantically

19

for assistance. But no one came to me. And even as I screamed the wall descended perpendicularly upon me and lay clammily upon my chest. An odour of corruption surged from it and when I tore at it with my fingers it made a low, gurgling sound, which gradually increased in volume till it woke echoes in the low-vaulted ceiling.

"The thing had pinioned my arms, and the more I twisted and squirmed the more agonizingly it tightened about me. The constriction increased until breathing became a torture, until all my flesh palpitated with pain. I wriggled and twisted, and bit my lips through in an extremity of horror.

"Then, abruptly, the pressure ceased and I became aware of two unblinking, fish-white eyes glaring truculently at me through the darkness. Agonizingly I sat up and ran my hands over my chest and arms. My fingers encountered a warm wetness and with a hideous clarity it was borne in on me that the thing had been feasting on my blood! The revelation was very close to mind-shattering. I was on my feet in an instant, trying desperately not to succumb to panic, but knowing, deep in my mind, that it would be a losing battle.

"A most awful terror was upon me, and so unreasoning became my desire to escape from that fearsome, vampirish obscenity that I retreated straight toward the throne of Chaugnar Faugn.

"It loomed enormous in the darkness, a refuge and a sanctuary. The wild thought came to me that if I could scale the throne and climb upon the lap of the god the horror might cease to molest me. Malignant beyond belief it undoubtedly was. But I refused to credit it with more than animalistic intelligence. Even in that moment of infinite peril, as I groped shakingly toward the rear of the cave, my mind was evolving a conceit to account for it.

"It was undoubtedly, I told myself, some cave-lurking survival from the age of reptiles—some atavistic and predatory abnormality that had experienced no necessity to advance on the course of evolution. It is more than probable that all backboned animals above the level of fishes and amphibians originated in Asia, and I had recklessly conveyed myself to the hoariest section of that primeval continent. Was it after all so amazing that I should have encountered, in a dark and inaccessible cave on a virtually uninhabited plateau, a reptilian predator endowed with the rapacity of that most hideous of bloodsucking animals—the vampire bat of the tropics?

"It was a just-short-of-destructive conceit and it sustained me and made my desperate groping for some kind of certainty seem the opposite of wasted until I reached the throne of Great Chaugnar. I fear that up to that instant my failure to suspect the truth was downright idiotic. There was only one adequate explanation for what had occurred. But it wasn't until I actually ascended the throne and began to feel about in the darkness for the body of Chaugnar that the truth rushed in upon me.

"Great Chaugnar had forsaken its throne! It had descended into the cave and was roaming about in the darkness. In its vampirish explorations it had stumbled upon my sleeping form, and had felled me with its trunk so that it might satisfy its thirst for blood with quick and hideous ferocity.

"For an instant I crouched motionless upon the stone, screaming inwardly, feeling the darkness tightening about me like a shroud. Then, quickly, I began to descend. But

I had not lowered more than my right leg when something ponderous collided with the base of the throne. The entire structure shook and I was almost hurled to the ground.

"I refuse to dwell on what happened after that. There are experiences too revolting for sane description. Were I to tell how the horror began slowly, to mount, to recount at length how it heaved its slabby and mucid vastness to the pinnacle of its throne and began nauseatingly to breathe upon me, the slight uncertainty I now entertain as to my sanity would be dispelled in short order.

"Neither shall I describe how it picked me up in its corpse-cold hands and began detestably to maul me, and how I nearly fainted beneath the foulness which drooled from its mouth. Eventually it wearied of its malign sport. After sinking its slimy black nails into my throat and chest until the pain became almost unbearable, it experienced a sudden excess of wrath and hurled me violently from the pedestal.

"The fall stunned me and for many minutes I lay on my back on the stones, dimly conscious only of a furtive whispering in the darkness about me. Then, slowly, my vision cleared and under the guidance of some nebulous and sinister influence my eyes were drawn upward until they encountered the pedestal from which I had fallen and the enormous, ropy bulk of Chaugnar Faugn loathsomely waving his great trunk in the dawn.

"It isn't surprising that when Chung Ga found me deliriously gibbering at the cavern's mouth he was obliged to carry me into the sunlight and force great wooden spoonfuls of revivifying wine down my parched throat. If there was *anything* inexplicable in the sequel to that hideous nightmare it was the matter-of-fact reception which he accorded my story.

"He nodded his head sympathetically when I recounted my experiences on the throne, and assured me that the incident accorded splendidly with the prophecies of Mu Sang. 'I was afraid,' he said, 'that Great Chaugnar would not accept you as its companion and nurse—that it would destroy you as utterly as it has the guardians—more of the guardians than you might suppose, for a god is not motivated by our kind of expediency.'

"He studied me for a moment intensely. 'No doubt you think me a superstitious savage, a ridiculous barbarian. Would it surprise you very much if I should tell you that I have spent eight years in England and that I am a graduate of the University of Oxford?'

"I could only stare at him in stunned disbelief for a moment, but so unbelievable and ghastly had been the coming to life of Chaugnar Faugn that lesser wonders made little impression on me and my incredulity passed quickly. Had he told me that he had an eye in the middle of his back or a tail twenty feet long which he kept continuously coiled about his body I should have evinced little surprise. I doubt indeed if anything short of a universal cataclysm could have roused me from my dazed acceptance of revelations which, under ordinary circumstances, I should have dismissed as preposterous.

" 'It astonishes you perhaps that I should have cast my lot with filthy primitives in this loathsome place and that I should have so uncompromisingly menaced your countrymen.' A wistfulness crept into his eyes. 'Your Richardson was a brave man. Even Chaugnar Faugn was moved to compassion by his valour. He gave no cry when we drove

23

wooden stakes through his hands and impaled him. For three days he defied us. Then Chaugnar tramped toward him in the night and set him at liberty.

" 'You may be sure that from that instant we accorded him every consideration. But to return to what you would undoubtedly call my perverse and atavistic attitude. Why do you suppose I chose to serve Chaugnar?'

"His recapitulation of what he had done to Richardson had awakened in me a confused but violent resentment. 'I don't know,' I muttered. 'There are degrees of human vileness—'

" 'Spare me your opprobrium, I beg of you,' he exclaimed. 'It was Great Chaugnar speaking through me that dictated the fate of Richardson. I am merely Chaugnar's interpreter and instrument. For generations my forebears have served Chaugnar, and I have never attempted to evade the duties that were delegated to me when our world was merely a thought in the mind of my god. I went to England and acquired a little of the West's decadent culture merely that I might more worthily serve Chaugnar.

" 'Don't imagine for a moment that Chaugnar is a beneficent god. In the West you have evolved certain amiabilities of intercourse, to which you presumptuously attach cosmic significance, such as truth, kindliness, generosity, forbearance and honour, and you quaintly imagine that a god who is beyond good and evil and hence unamenable to your "ethics" can not be omnipotent.

" 'But how do you know that there *are* any beneficent laws in the universe, that the cosmos is friendly to man? Even in the mundane sphere of planetary life there is nothing to sustain such an hypothesis.

24

" 'Great Chaugnar is a terrible god, an utterly cosmic and unanthropomorphic god. It is akin to the fire mists and the primordial ooze, and before it incarned itself in Time it contained within itself the past, the present and the future. Nothing was and nothing will be, but all things are. And Chaugnar Faugn was once the sum of all things that are.'

"I remained silent and a note of compassion crept into his voice. I think he perceived that I had no inclination to split hairs with him over the paradoxes of transcendental metaphysics.

" 'Chaugnar Faugn,' he continued, 'did not always dwell in the East. Many thousands of years ago it abode with its Brothers in a cave in Western Europe, and made from the flesh of toads a race of small dark shapes to serve it. In bodily contour these shapes resembled men, but they were incapable of speech and their thoughts were the thoughts of Chaugnar.

" 'The cave where Chaugnar dwelt was never visited by men, for it wound its twisted length through a high and inaccessible crag of the mysterious Pyrenees, and all the regions beneath were rife with abominable hauntings.

" 'Twice a year Chaugnar Faugn sent its servants into the villages that dotted the foothills to bring it the sustenance its belly craved. The chosen youths and maidens were preserved with spices and stored in the cave till Chaugnar had need of them. And in the villages men would hurl their first-borns into the flames and offer prayers to their futile little gods, hoping thereby to appease the wrath of Chaugnar's mindless servants.

" 'But eventually there came into the foothills men like gods, stout, eagle-visaged men who carried on their shields the insignia of invincible Rome. They scaled the mountains in pursuit of the servants and awoke a cosmic foreboding in the mind of Chaugnar.

" 'It is true that its Brethren succeeded without difficulty in exterminating the impious cohorts—exterminating them unspeakably—before they reached the cave, but it feared that rumours of the attempted sacrilege would bring legions of the empire-builders into the hills and then eventually its sanctuary would be defiled.

" 'So in ominous conclave it debated with its Brothers the advisability of flight. Rome was but a dream in the mind of Chaugnar and it could have destroyed her utterly in an instant, but having incarned itself in Time it did not wish to resort to violence until the prophecies were fulfilled.

" 'Chaugnar and its Brothers conversed by means of thought-transference in an idiom incomprehensible to us and it would be both dangerous and futile to attempt to repeat the exact substance of their discourse. But it is recorded in the prophecy of Mu Sang that Great Chaugnar spoke *approximately* as follows:

" ' "Our servants shall carry us eastward to the primal continent, and there we shall await the arrival of the White Acolyte."

" 'His Brothers demurred. "We are safe here," they affirmed. "No one will scale the mountains again, for the doom that came to Pompelo will reverberate in the dreams of prophets till Rome is less to be feared than moon-dim Ninevah, or Medusa-girdled Ur."

" 'At that Great Chaugnar waxed ireful and affirmed that it would go alone to the primal continent, leaving its Brothers to cope with the menace of Rome. "When the

26

time-frames are dissolved I alone shall ascend in glory," it told them. "All of you I shall devour before I ascend to the dark altars. When the hour of my transfiguration approaches you will come down from the mountains cosmically athirst for That Which is Not to be Spoken of, but even as your bodies raven for the time-dissolving sacrament I shall consume them. "

" 'Then it called for the servants and had them carry it to this place. And it caused Mu Sang to be born from the womb of an ape and the prophecies to be written on imperishable parchment, and into the care of my fathers it surrendered its body.'

"I rose gropingly to my feet. 'Let me leave this place,' I pleaded. 'I respect your beliefs and I give you my solemn word I will never attempt to return. Your secrets are safe with me. Only let me go—'

"Chung Ga's features were convulsed with pity. 'It is stated in the prophecy that you must be Chaugnar's companion and accompany it to America. In a few days it will experience a desire to feed again. You must nurse it unceasingly.'

" 'I am ill,' I pleaded. 'I can not carry Chaugnar Faugn across the desert plateau.'

" 'I will have the guardians assist you,' murmured Chung Ga soothingly. 'You shall be conveyed in comfort to the gates of Lhasa, and from Lhasa to the coast it is less than a week's journey by caravan.'

"I realized then how impossible it would be for me to depart without Great Chaugnar. 'Very well, Chung Ga,' I said. 'I submit to the prophecy. Chaugnar shall be my companion and I shall nurse it as diligently as it desires.'

"There was a ring of insincerity in my speech which was not lost on Chung Ga. He approached very close to me and peered into my eyes. 'If you attempt to dispose of my god,' he warned, 'its Brothers will come down from the mountains and tear you indescribably.'

"He saw perhaps that I wasn't wholly convinced, for he added in an even more ominous tone, 'It has laid upon you the mark and seal of a flesh-dissolving sacrament. Destroy it, and the sacrament will be consummated in an instant. The flesh of your body will turn black and melt like tallow in the sun. You will become a seething mass of corruption.' "

Ulman paused, a look of unutterable torment in his eyes. "There isn't much more to my story, Algernon. The guardians carried us safely to Lhasa and a fortnight later I reached the Bay of Bengal, accompanied by half a hundred ragged, gaunt-visaged mendicants from the temples of obscure Indian villages. There was something about our caravan that had attracted them. And all during the voyage from Bengal to Hong Kong the Indian and Tibetan members of our crew would steal stealthily to my cabin at night and look in on me, and I had never before seen human faces quite so distorted with superstitious terror.

"Don't imagine for a moment that I didn't share their awe and fear of the thing I was compelled to companion. Continuously I longed to carry it on deck and cast it into the sea. Only the memory of Chung Ga's warning and the thought of what might happen to me if I disregarded it kept me chained and submissive.

"It was not until weeks later, when I had left the Indian and most of the Pacific Ocean behind me, that I discovered how unwise I had been to heed his vile threats. If I had resolutely hurled Chaugnar into the sea the shame and the horror might never have come upon me! "

Ulman's voice was rising, becoming shrill and hysterical. "Chaugnar Faugn is an awful and mysterious being, a repellent and obscene and lethal being, but how do I know that it is omnipotent? Chung Ga may have maliciously lied to me. Chaugnar Faugn may be merely an extension or distortion of inanimate nature. Some hideous *process,* as yet unobserved and unexplained by the science of the West, may be obnoxiously at work in desert places all over our planet to produce such fiendish anomalies. Perhaps parallel to protoplasmic life on the earth's crust is this other aberrant and hidden life—the revolting sentiency of stones that aspire, of earth-shapes, parasitic and bestial, that wax agile in the presence of man.

"Did not Cuvier believe that there had been not one but an infinite number of 'creations,' and that as our earth cooled after its departure from the sun a succession of vitalic phenomena appeared on its surface? Conceding as we must the orderly and continuous development of proto-plasmic life from simple forms, which Cuvier stupidly and ridiculously denied, is it not still conceivable that another evolutionary cycle may have preceded the one which has culminated in us? A non-protoplasmic cycle?

"Whether we accept the planetismal or the three or four newer theories of planetary formation it is permissible to believe that the earth coalesced very swiftly into a compact mass after the segregation of its constituents in space and that it achieved sufficient crustal stability to support animate entities one, or two, or perhaps even five billion years ago.

"I do not claim that life *as we know it* would be possible

to assert dogmatically that beings possessed of intelligence and volition could not have evolved in a direction merely parallel to the cellular? Life as we know it is complexly bound up with such substances as chlorophyll and protoplasm, but does that preclude that possibility of an evolved sentiency in other forms of matter?

"How do we know that stones cannot think; that the earth beneath our feet may not once have been endowed with a hideous intelligence? Entire cycles of animate evolution may have occurred on this planet before the most primitive of 'living' cells were evolved from the slime of warm seas.

"There may have been eons of—experiments! Three billion years ago in the fiery radiance of rapidly condensing earth who knows what monstrous shapes crawled—or shambled?

"And how do we know that there are not survivals? Or that somewhere beneath the stars of heaven complex and hideous processes are not still at work, shaping the inorganic into forms of primal malevolence?

"And what more inevitable than some such primiparous spawn should have become in my eyes the apotheosis of all that was fiendish and accursed and unclean, and that I should have ascribed to it the attributes of divinity, and imagined in a moment of madness that it was immune to destruction? I should have hurled it into the depths of the seas and risked boldly the fulfilment of Chung Ga's prophecy. For even had it proved itself omnipotent and omniscient by rising in fury from the waves or summoning its Brothers to destroy me I should have suffered indescribably for no more than a moment."

Ulman's voice had risen to a shrill scream. "I should have passed quickly enough into the darkness had I encountered merely the wrath of Chaugnar Faugn. It was not the fury but the forbearance of Chaugnar that has wrought an uncleanliness in my body's flesh, and blackened and shrivelled my soul, till a furious hate has grown up in for all that the world holds of serenity and joy."

Ulman's voice broke and for a moment there was silence in the room. Then, with a sudden, convulsive movement of his right arm he uncloaked the whole of his face.

He was standing very nearly in the centre of the office and the light from its eastern window illumed with a hideous clarity all that remained of his features. But Algernon didn't utter a sound, for all that the sight was appalling enough to revolt a corpse. He simply clung shakingly to the desk and waited with ashen lips for Ulman to continue.

"It came to me again as I slept, drinking its fill, and in the morning I woke to find that the flesh of my body had grown fetid and loathsome, and that my face—my face . . ."

"Yes, Clark, I understand." Algernon's voice was vibrant with compassion. "I'll get you some brandy."

Ulman's eyes shown with an awful light.

"Do you believe me?" he cried. "Do you believe that Chaugnar Faugn has wrought this uncleanliness?"

Slowly Algernon shook his head. "No, Clark, Chaugnar Faugn is nothing but a stone idol, sculptured by some Asian artist with quite exceptional talent, however primitive he may have been in other respects. I believe that Chung Ga kept you under the influence of some potent drug until he had—had cut your face, and that he also hypnotized you and suggested every detail of the story you

31

have just told me. I believe you are still actually under the spell of that hypnosis."

"When I boarded the ship at Calcutta there was nothing wrong with my face!" shrilled Ulman.

"Conceivably not. But some minion of the priest may have administered the drug and performed the operation on shipboard. I can only guess at what happened, of course, but it is obvious that you are the victim of some hideous charlatanry. I've visited India, Clark, and I have a very keen respect for the hypnotic endowments of the Oriental. It's ghastly and unbelievable how much a Hindoo or a Tibetan can accomplish by simple suggestion."

"I feared—I feared that you would doubt!" Ulman's voice had risen to a shriek. "But I swear to you . . ."

The sentence was never finished. A hideous pallor overspread the archaeologist's face, his jaw sagged and into his eyes there crept a look of panic fight. For a second he stood clawing at his throat, like a man in the throes of an epileptic fit.

Then something, some invisible force, seemed to propel him backward. Choking and gasping he staggered against the wall and threw out his arms in a gesture of frantic appeal. "Keep it off!" he sobbed. "I can't breathe. I can't . . ."

With a cry Algernon leapt forward, but before he reached the other's side the unfortunate man had sunk to the floor and was moaning and gibbering and rolling about in a most sickening way.

2. The Atrocity at the Museum

ALGERNON HARRIS emerged from the B. M. T. subway at the Fifty-ninth Street and Fifth Avenue entrance and began nervously to pace the sidewalk in front of a large yellow sign, which bore the discouraging caption: "Buses do not stop here." Harris was most eager to secure a bus and it was obvious from the expectant manner in which he hailed the first one to pass that he hadn't the faintest notion he had taken up his post on the wrong side of the street. Indeed, it was not until four buses had passed him by that he awoke to the gravity of his predicament and began to propel his person in the direction of the legitimate stop-zone.

Algernon Harris was abnormally and tragically upset. But even a man trembling on the verge of a neuropathic collapse can remain superficially politic, and it isn't surprising that when he ascended into his bus and encountered on a conspicuous seat his official superior, Doctor George Francis Scollard, he should have nodded, smiled and responded with an unwavering amiability to the questions that were shot at him.

33

"I got your telegram yesterday," murmured the president of the Manhattan Museum of Fine Arts, "and I caught the first train down. Am I too late for the inquest?"

Algernon nodded. "The coroner—a chap named Henry Weigal—took my evidence and rendered a decision on the spot. The condition of Ulman's body would not have permitted of delay. I never before imagined that—that putrefaction could proceed with such incredible rapidity."

Scollard frowned. "And the verdict?"

"Heart failure. The coroner was very positive that anxiety and shock were the sole causes of Ulman's total collapse."

"But you said something about his face being horribly disfigured."

"Yes. It had been rendered loathsome by—by plastic surgery. Weigal was hideously agitated until I explained that Ulman had merely fallen into the hands of a skilful Oriental surgeon with sadistic inclination in the course of his archaeological explorations. I explained to him that many of our field workers returned slightly disfigured and that Ulman had merely endured an exaggeration of the customary martyrdom."

"And you believe that plastic surgery could account for the repellent and gruesome changes you mentioned in your nightletter—the shocking prolongation of the poor devil's nose, the flattening and broadening of his ears . . ."

Algernon winced. "I must believe it, sir. It is impossible sanely to entertain any other explanation. The coroner's assistant was a little incredulous at first, until Weigal pointed out to him what an unwholesome precedent they would set by even so much as hinting that the phenomenon wasn't pathologically explicable. 'We would play right into the hands of the spiritualists,' Weigal explained. 'An officer of the police isn't at liberty to adduce an hypothesis that the district attorney's office wouldn't approve of. The newspapers would pounce on a thing like that and play it up disgustingly. Mr. Harris has supplied us with an explanation which seems adequately to cover the facts, and with your permission I shall file a verdict of natural death.' "

The president coughed and shifted uneasily in his seat. "I am glad that the coroner took such a sensible view of the matter. Had he been a recalcitrant individual and raised objections we should have come in for considerable unpleasant publicity. I shudder whenever I see a reference to the Museum in the popular press. It is always the morbid and sensational aspects of our work that they stress and there is never the slightest attention paid to accuracy."

For a long moment Dr. Scollard was silent. Then he cleared his throat, and recapitulated, in a slightly more emphatic form, the question that he had put to Algernon originally. "But you said in your letter that Ulman's nose revolted and sickened you—that it had become a loathsome greenish trunk almost a foot in length which continued to move about for hours after Ulman's heart stopped beating. Could—could your operation hypothesis account for such an appalling anomaly?"

Algernon took a deep breath. "I can't pretend that I wasn't astounded and appalled and—and frightened. And so lost to discretion that I made no attempt to conceal the way I felt from the coroner. I could not remain in the room while they were examining the body."

"And yet you succeeded in convincing the coroner that he could justifiably render a verdict of natural death!"

"You misunderstood me, sir. The coroner *wanted* to render such a verdict. My explanation merely supplied him with a straw to clutch at. I was trembling in every limb when I made it and it must have been obvious to him that we were in the presence of something unthinkable. But without the plastic surgery assumption we should have had nothing whatever to cling to."

"And do you still give your reluctant assent to such an assumption?"

"Now more than ever. And my assent is no longer reluctant, for I've succeeded in convincing myself that a surgeon endowed with miraculous skill could have effected the transformation I described in my letter."

"Miraculous skill?"

"I use the word in a merely mundane sense. When one stops to consider what astounding advances plastic surgery has made in England and America during the past decade it is impossible to disbelieve that the human frame will soon become more malleable than wax beneath the scalpels of our surgeons and that beings will appear in our midst with bodies so grotesquely distorted that the superstitious will ascribe their advent to the supernatural.

"And we can adduce *more* than a surgical 'miracle' to account for the horror that poor Ulman became without for a moment encroaching on the dubious domain of the super-physical. Every one knows how extensively the duct-less glands regulate the growth and shape of our bodies. A change in the quantity or quality of secretion in any one of the glands may throw the entire human mechanism out of gear. Terrible and unthinkable changes have been known to occur in the adult body during the course of diseases involving glandular instability. We once thought

36

that human beings invariably ceased to grow at twenty-one or twenty-two, but we now know that growth may continue till middle age, and even till the very onset of senility, and that frequently such growth does not culminate in a mere increase in stature or in girth.

"Doubtless you have heard of that rare, and hideously deforming glandular malady acromegaly. It is characterized by an abnormal over-growth of the skull and face, and the small bones of the extremities, and its victims become in a short time tragic caricatures of humanity. The entire face assumes a more massive cast but the over-growth is most pronounced in the region of the jawbones. In exceptional cases the face has been known to attain a length of nearly a foot. But it is not so much the size as the revolting primitiveness of the face which sets the victims of this hideous disease so tragically apart from their fellows. The features not only grow, but they take on an almost ape-like aspect, and as the disease advances even the skull becomes revoltingly simian in its conformation. In brief, the victims of acromegaly become in a short while almost indistinguishable from very primitive and brutish types of human ancestors, such as *Homo neanderthalensis* and the unmentionable, enormous-browed caricature from Broken Hill, Rhodesia, which Sir Arthur Keith has called the most unqualifiedly repulsive physiognomy in the entire gallery of fossil men.

"The disease of acromegaly is perhaps a more certain indication of man's origin than all the 'missing links' that anthropologists have exhumed. It proves incontestably that we still carry within our bodies the mechanism of evolutionary retrogression, and that when something interferes with the normal functioning of our glands we are very apt to return, at least physically, to our aboriginal status.

"And since we know that a mere insufficiency or super-abundance of glandular secretions can work such devastating changes, can turn men virtually into Neanderthalers, or great apes, what is there really unaccountable in the alteration I witnessed in poor Ulman?

"Some Oriental diabolist merely ten years in advance of the West in the sphere of plastic surgery and with a knowledge of glandular therapeutics no greater than that possessed by Doctors Noel Paton and Schafer might easily have wrought such an abomination. Or suppose, as I have hinted before, that no surgery was involved, suppose that this fiend has learned so much about our glands that he can send men back and back through the mists of time—back past the great apes and the primitive mammals and the carnivorous dinosaurs to their primordial sires! Suppose—it is an awful thought, I know—suppose that some creature closely resembling what Ulman became was *once* our ancestor, that a hundred million years ago a gigantic batrachian shape with trunklike appendages and great flapping ears paddled through the warm primeval seas or stretched its leathery length on banks of Permian slime! "

Dr. Scollard turned sharply and plucked at his subordinate's sleeve. "There's a crowd in front of the Museum," he muttered. "See there! "

Algernon started, and rising instantly, pressed the signal bell above his companion's head. "We'll have to walk back," he muttered despondently. "I should have watched the street numbers."

His pessimism proved well-founded. The bus continued relentlessly on its way for four additional blocks and then

38

came so abruptly to a stop that Dr. Scollard was subjected to the ignominy of being obliged to sit for an instant on the spacious lap of a middle-aged stout woman who resented the encroachment with a furious glare.

"I've a good mind to report you," he shouted to the bus conductor as he lowered his portly person to the sidewalk. "I've a damn good mind . . ."

"Let it pass, sir." Algernon laid a pacifying arm on his companion's arm. "We've got no time to argue. Something dreadful has occurred at the Museum. I just saw two policemen enter the building. And those tall men walking up and down on the opposite side of the street are reporters. There's Wells of the *Tribune* and Thompson of the *Times*, and . . ."

Dr. Scollard gripped his subordinate's arm. "Tell me," he demanded, "did you put the—the statue on *exhibition?*"

Algernon nodded. "I had it carried to Alcove K, Wing C last night. After the inquest on poor Ulman I was besieged by reporters. They wanted to know all about the fetish, and of course I had to tell them that it would go on exhibition eventually. They would have returned very day for weeks to pester me if I hadn't assured them that we'd respect the public clamour to that extent at least.

"Yesterday afternoon all the papers ran specials about it. The *News-Graphic* gave it a front-page write-up. I remained at my office until eleven, and all evening at half-minute intervals some emotionally overcharged numskull would ring up and ask me when I was going to exhibit the thing and whether it really looked as repulsive as its photographs, and what kind of stone it was made of and— oh, God! I was too nervous and wrought-up to be bothered that way and I decided it would be best to satisfy the

39

public's idiotic curiosity by permitting them to view the thing today."

The two men were walking briskly in the direction of the Museum.

"Besides, there was no longer any necessity of my keeping it in the office. I had had it measured and photographed and I knew that Harrison and Smithstone wouldn't want to take a cast of it until next week. And I couldn't have chosen a safer place for it than Alcove K. It's roped off, you know, and only two paces removed from the door. Cinney can see it all night from his station in the corridor."

By the time that Algernon and Dr. Scollard arrived at the Museum the crowd had reached alarming proportions. They were obliged to fight their way through a solid phalanx of excited men and women who impeded their progress with elbow-thrusting aggressiveness, and scant respect for their dignity. And even in the vestibules they were repulsed with discourtesy.

A red-headed policeman glared savagely at them from behind horn-rimmed spectacles and brought them to a halt with a threatening gesture. "You've got to keep out!" he shouted. "If you ain't got a police card you've got to keep out!"

"What's happened here?" demanded Algernon authoritatively.

"A guy's been bumped off. If you ain't got a police card you've got to . . ."

Algernon produced a calling-card and thrust it into the officer's face. "I'm the curator of archaeology," he affirmed angrily. "I guess I've got a right to enter my own museum."

The officer's manner softened perceptibly. "Then I guess

it's all right. The chief told me I wasn't to keep out any of the guys that work here. How about your friend?"

"You can safely admit him," murmured Algernon with a smile. "He's president of the Museum."

The policeman did not seem too astonished. He regarded Dr. Scollard dubiously for a moment. Then he shrugged his shoulders and stepped complacently aside.

An attendant greeted them excitedly as they emerged from the turnstile. "It's awful, sir," he gasped, addressing Dr. Scollard. "Cinney has been murdered—knifed, sir. He's all cut and mangled. I shouldn't have recognized him if it weren't for his clothes. There's nothing left on his face, sir."

Algernon turned pale. "When—when did this happen?" he gasped.

The attendant shook his head. "I can't say, Mr. Harris. It must've been some time last night, but I can't say exactly when. The first we knew of it was when Mr. Williams came running down the stairs with his hands all bloodied. That was at eight this morning, about two hours ago. I'd just got in, and all the other attendants were in the cloak room getting into their uniforms. That is, all except Williams. Williams usually arrives about a half-hour before the rest of us. He likes to come early and have a chat with Cinney before the doors open."

The attendant's face was convulsed with terror and he spoke with considerable difficulty. "I was the only one to see him come down the stairs. I was standing about here and as soon as he came into sight I knew that something was wrong with him. He went from side to side of the stairs and clung to the rails to keep himself from falling. And his face was as white as paper."

41

Algernon's eyes did not leave the attendant's face. "Go on," he urged.

"He opened his mouth very wide when he saw me. It was like as if he wanted to shout and couldn't. There wasn't a sound came out of him."

The attendant cleared his throat. "I didn't think he'd ever reach the bottom of the stairs and I called out for the boys in the cloak room to lend me a hand."

"What happened then?"

"He didn't speak for a long time. One of the boys gave him some whisky out of a flask and the rest of us just stood about and said soothing things to him. But he was trembling all over and we couldn't quiet him down. He kept throwing his head about pointing toward the stairs. And foam collected all over his mouth. It was ghastly.

" 'What's wrong, Jim?' I said to him. 'What did you see?'

" 'The worm of hell!' he said. 'The Devil's awful mascot!' He said other things I can't repeat, sir. I'm a God-fearing man, and there are blasphemies it's best to forget you ever heard. But I'll tell you what he said when he got through talking about the worm out of hell. He said: 'Cinney's upstairs stretched out on his back and there ain't a drop of blood in his veins.'

"We got up the stairs quicker than lightning after he'd told us that. We didn't know just what his crazy words meant, but the blood on his hands made us sure that something pretty terrible had happened. They kind of confirmed what we feared, sir—if you get what I mean."

Algernon nodded. "And you found Cinney—dead?"

"Worse than that, sir. All black and shrunken and looking as though he'd been wearing clothes about four sizes too large for him. His face was all *gone*, sir—all eaten away, like. We picked him up—he wasn't much heavier than a little boy—and laid him out on a bench in Corridor H. I never seen so much blood in my life—the floor was all slippery with it. And the big stone animal you had us carry down to Alcove K last night was all dripping with it, 'specially its trunk. It made me sort of sick. I never like to look at blood."

"You think someone attacked Cinney?"

"It looked that way, Mr. Harris. Like as if some one went for him with a knife. It must have been an awful big knife—a regular butcher's knife. That ain't a very nice way of putting it, sir, but that's how it struck me. Like as if some one mistook him for a piece of mutton."

"And what else did you find when you examined him?"

"We didn't do much examining. We just let him lie on the bench till we got through phoning for the police. Mr. Williams did all the talking, sir." A look of relief crept into the attendant's eyes. "The police said we wasn't to disturb the body further, which suited us fine. There wasn't one of us didn't want to give poor Mr. Cinney a wide berth."

"And what did the police do when they arrived?"

"Asked us about a million crazy questions, sir. Was Mr. Cinney disfigured in the war? And was Mr. Cinney in the habit of wearing a mask over his face? And had Mr. Cinney received any threatening letters from Chinamen or Hindoos? And when we told them no, they seemed to get kind of frightened. 'If it ain't murder,' they said, 'we're up against something that ain't natural. But it's got to be murder. All we have to do is get hold of the Chinaman.'"

Algernon didn't wait to hear more. Brushing the

43

attendant ungratefully aside he went dashing up the stairs three steps at a time. Dr. Scollard followed with ashen face.

They were met in the upper corridor by a tall, loose-jointed man in shabby, ill-fitting clothes who arrested their progress with a scowl and a torrent of impatient abuse. "Where do you think you're going?" he demanded. "Didn't I give orders that no one was to come up here? I've got nothing to say to you. You're too damn nosy. If you want the lowdown on this affair you've got to wait outside till we get through questioning the attendants."

"See here," said Algernon impatiently. "This gentleman is president of the Museum and he has a perfect right to go where he chooses."

The tall man waxed apologetic. "I thought you were a couple of newspaper Johns," he murmured confusedly. "We haven't anything even remotely resembling a clue, but those guys keep popping in here every ten minutes to cross-examine us. They're worse than prosecuting attorneys. Come right this way, sir."

He led them past a little knot of attendants and photographers and fingerprint experts to the northerly part of the corridor. "There's the body," he said, pointing toward a sheeted form which lay sprawled on a low bench near the window. "I'd be grateful if you gentlemen would look at the poor lad's face."

Algernon nodded, and lifting a corner of the sheet peered for an instant intently into what remained of poor Cinney's countenance. Then, with a shudder, he surrendered his place to Dr. Scollard.

It is to Dr. Scollard's credit that he did not cry out. Only

44

the trembling of his lower lip betrayed the revulsion which filled him.

"He was found on the floor in the corridor about two hours ago," explained the detective. "But the guy who found him isn't here. They've got him in a straitjacket down at Bellevue, and it doesn't look as though he'll be much help to us. He was yelling his head off about something he said came out of hell when they put him in the ambulance. That's what drew the crowd."

"You don't think Williams could have done it?" murmured Algernon.

"Not a chance. But he saw the murderer all right, and if we can get him to talk . . ." He wheeled on Algernon abruptly. "You seem to know something about this, sir."

"Only what we picked up downstairs. We had a talk with one of the attendants and he explained about Williams—and the Chinaman."

The detective's eyes glowed. "The Chinaman? What Chinaman? Is there a Chinaman mixed up in this? It's what I've been thinking all along, but I didn't have much to go on."

"I fear we're becoming involved in a vicious circle," said Algernon. "It was your Chinaman I was referring to. Willy said you were labouring under the impression that all you had to do to solve this distressing affair was to catch a Chinaman."

The detective shook his head. "It's not as simple as that," he affirmed. "We haven't any positive evidence that a Chinaman did it. It might have been a Jap or Hindoo or even a South Sea Islander. That is, if South Sea Islanders eat rice! "

"Rice?" Algernon stared at the detective incredulously.

"That's right. In a bowl with long sticks. I'm no authority on et-eternalogy, but it's my guess they don't use chopsticks much outside of Asia."

He went into Alcove K and returned with a wooden bowl and two long splinters of wood. "All those dark spots near the rim are blood stains," he explained, as he surrendered the gruesome exhibits to Algernon. "Even the rice is all smeared with blood." Algernon shuddered and passed the bowl to Scollard, who almost dropped it in his haste to return it to the detective.

"Where did you find it?" The president spoke in a subdued whisper.

"On the floor in front of the big stone elephant. That's where Cinney was killed. There's blood all over the elephant—if it's supposed to be an elephant."

"It isn't, strictly speaking, an elephant," said Algernon.

"Well, whatever it is, it could tell us what Cinney's murderer looked like. I'd give the toes off my left foot if it could talk."

"It doesn't talk," said Algernon decisively.

"I wasn't wisecracking," admonished the detective. "I was simply pointing out that that elephant could give up the lowdown on a might nasty murder."

Algernon accepted the rebuke in silence.

"There ain't no doubt whatever that a Chinaman or Hindoo or some crazy foreigner sneaked in here last night, set himself down in front of that elephant and began eating rice. Maybe he was in a church-going mood and mistook the beast for one of his heathen gods. It kind of looks like an oriental idol—the ferocious-looking kind you sometimes see in Chinatown store windows."

Algernon smiled ironically. "But unquestionably unique," he murmured.

The detective nodded. "Yeah. Larger and uglier-looking, but a heathen statue for all that. I bet it actually was worshipped once. Hindu . . . Chinese . . . I wouldn't know. But it sure has that look."

"Yes," admitted Algernoon, "it is indubitably in the religious tradition. For all its hideousness it has all the earmarks of a quiescent Eastern divinity."

"There ain't anything more dangerous than interfering with an Oriental when he's saying his prayers," continued the detective. "I've been in Chinatown raids, and I know. Now here's what I think happened. Cinney is standing in the corridor and suddenly he hears the Chinaman muttering and mumbling to himself in the dark. He's naturally frightened and so he rushes in with his pocketlight where an angel would be fearing to tread. The light gets in the Chinaman's eyes and sets him off.

"It's like putting a match to a ton of TNT to throw a light on a Chinaman when he's squatting in the dark in a worshipful mood. So the Chinaman goes for the kid with a knife. He feels outraged in a religious way, isn't really himself, thinks he's avenging an insult to the idol."

Algernoon nodded impatiently. "There may be something in your theory, sergeant. But there's a great deal it doesn't explain. What was it that Williams saw?"

"Nothing but Cinney lying dead in the corridor. Nothing but Cinney looking up at him without a face and that awful heathen animal looking down at him with blood all over its mouth."

Algernon stared. "Blood on its mouth?"

"Sure. All over its mouth, trunk and tusks. Never seen

47

so much blood in my life. That's what Williams saw. I don't wonder it crumpled the kid up."

There was a commotion in the corridor. Someone was sobbing and pleading in a most fantastic way a few yards from where the three men were standing. The detective turned and shouted a curt command. "Whoever that is, bring him here!"

Came an appalling, ear-harassing shriek and two plain-clothesmen emerged around a bend in the corridor with a dimunitive and weeping Oriental spread-eagled between their extended arms.

"The Chinaman!" muttered Scollard in amazement.

For a second the detective was too startled to move, and his immobility somehow emboldened the Chinese to break from his captors and prostrate himself on the floor at Algernon's feet.

"You are my friend," he sobbed. "You are a very good man. I saw you in green-fire dream. In dream when big green animals came down from mountain I saw you and Gautama Siddhartha. Big green animals all wanted blood —all very much wanted blood. In dream Gautama Siddhartha said: 'They want you! They have determined they make you all dark fire glue.'

"I said, 'No! *Please*,' I said. Then Gautama Siddhartha let fall jewel of wisdom. 'Go to *museum*. Go to big *museum* round block, and big green animal will eat you quick. He will eat you quick—before he make American man dark fire glue.'

"All night I have sat here. All night I said: 'Eat me. *Please!*' But big green animal slept till American man came. Then he moved. Very quickly he moved. He gave

48

American man very bad hug. American man screamed and big green animal drank all American man's blood."

The little Oriental was sobbing unrestrainedly. Algernon stooped and lifted him gently to his feet. "What is your name?" he asked, to soothe him. "Where do you live?"

"I'm boss big laundry down street," murmured the Chinaman. "My name is Hsieh Ho. I am a good man, like you."

"Where did you go when—when the elephant came to life?"

The Chinaman's lower lip trembled convulsively. "I hid back of big white lady."

In spite of the gravity of the situation Algernon couldn't repress a smile. The "big white lady" was a statue of Venus Erycine and so enormous was it that it occupied almost the whole of Alcove K. It was a perfect sanctuary, but there was something ludicrously incongruous in a Chinaman's seeking refuge in such a place.

One of the detectives, however, confirmed the absurdity. "That's why we found him, sir. He was lying on his back, wailing and groaning and making faces at the ceiling. He's our man, all right. We'll have the truth out of him in ten minutes."

The chief sergeant nodded. "You bet we will. Put the bracelets on him, Jim."

Reluctantly Algernon surrendered Hsieh Ho to his captors. "I suggest you treat him kindly," he said. "He had the misfortune to witness a ghastly and unprecedented exaggeration of what Eddington would call the random element in nature. But he's as destitute of criminal proclivities as Dr. Scollard here."

49

The detective raised his eyebrows. "I don't get it, sir. Are you suggesting we just hold him as a material witness?"

Algernon nodded. "If you try any of your revolting third-degree tactics on that poor little man you'll answer in court to my lawyer. Now, if you don't mind, I'll have a look at Alcove K."

The detective scowled. He wanted to tell Algernon to go to hell, but somehow the inflection of authority in the latter's voice glued the invective to his tongue, and with a surly shrug he escorted the group into the presence of Chaugnar Faugn.

Sanguinary baptism becomes some gods. Were the gracious figures of the Grecian pantheon to appear to us with blood upon their garments we should recoil in horror, but we should think the terrible Mithra or the heart-devouring Huitzilopochtli a trifle unconvincing if they came on our dreams untarnished by the ruddy vintage of sacrifice.

Algernon did not at first look directly at Chaugnar Faugn. He studied the tiled marble floor about the base of the idol and tried to make out in the gloom the precise spot where Cinney had lain. The attempt proved confusing. There were dark smudges on almost every other tile and they were nearly all of equal circumference.

"Right there is where he found the corpse," said the detective impatiently. "Right beneath the trunk of the elephant."

Algernon's blood ran cold. Slowly, very slowly, for he feared to confront what stood before him, he raised his eyes until they were level with the detective's shoulders. The detective's shoulders concealed a portion of Chaugnar Faugn, but all of the thing's right side and the extremity of its trunk were hideously visible to Algernon as he stared. He spoke no word. He did not even move. But all of the blood drained out of his lips, leaving them ashen.

Dr. Scollard was staring at his subordinate with frightened eyes. "You act as though—as though—good God, man, what is it?"

"It has moved its trunk!" Algernon's voice was vibrant with horror. "It has moved its trunk since—since yesterday. And most hideously. I can not be mistaken. Yesterday it was vertical—today it is in a slightly upraised position."

Dr. Scollard gasped. "Are you sure?" he muttered. "Are you absolutely certain that the trunk wasn't in that position when the god arrived here?"

"Yes. yes. Not until today. In the excitement no one has noticed it, but if you will call the attendants—wait!"

The president had started to do that very thing, but Algernon's admonition brought him up short. "I shouldn't have suggested that," he murmured in Scollard's ear. "The attendants mustn't be questioned. It's all too unutterably ghastly and inexplicable and—and mad. We've got to keep it out of the papers, seek a solution secretly. I know some one who may be able to help us. The police can't. That's obvious."

The detective was staring at them pityingly. "You gentlemen better get out of here," he said. "You aren't used to sights like this. When I was new at this game I made a lot of mistakes. I could hardly stand the sight of a dead man, for instance. Used to hurry things along when there was no real need for haste, which is just about the worst mistake you can make at the preliminary examination stage."

With an effort Algernon mastered his agitation. "You're right, sergeant," he said. "Dr. Scollard and I realize that

51

this business is a little too disturbing for sane contemplation. So we'll retire, as you suggest. But I must warn you again that you'd better think twice about treating poor Hsieh Ho as a convicted murderer."

In the corridor he drew Dr. Scollard aside and conversed for a moment urgently in a low voice. Then he approached the detective and handed him a card. "If you want me within the next few hours you'll find me at this address," he said. "Dr. Scollard is returning to his home in Brooklyn. You'll find his phone number in the directory, but I hope you won't disturb him unless something really grave turns up."

The detective nodded and read aloud the address on Algernon's card. "Dr. Henry C. Imbert, F.R.S., F.A.G.S."

"A friend of yours?" he asked impertinently.

Algernon nodded. "Yes, sergeant. The foremost American ethnologist. Ever hear of him?"

To Algernon's amazement the sergeant nodded. "Yes. I got kind of interested in eternalogy once. I was on a queer case about two years ago. An old lady got bumped off by a poisoned arrow and we had him in for a powwow. He's clever all right. He gave us all the dope soon as he saw the corpse. Said a little negro had done it—one of those African pigmies you read about. We followed up the tip and caught the murderer just as he was giving the little fellow a cyanide cigarette to smoke. He was a shrewd Italian. He got the pigmy in Africa, hid him in a room down on Houston Street and sent him out to rob and bump off old ladies. He was as spry as a monkey and could shinny up a drainpipe on the side of a house in ten seconds. If it hadn't been for Imbert we'd never have got our hands on the guy that owned him."

Dr. Scollard and Algernon descended the stairs together. But in the vestibule they parted, the president proceeding down the still crowded outer steps in the direction of a bus whilst Algernon sought his office in Wing W.

"When Imbert sees this," Algernon murmured, as he extracted a photograph of Chaugnar Faugn from his chaotically littered desk, "he'll be the most disturbed ethnologist that this planet has harboured since the Pleistocene Age."

3. *An Archaeological Digression*

"THE FIGURE is totally unfamiliar," said Doctor Imbert. "Nothing even remotely resembling it occurs in Asian or African mythology."

He scowled and returned the photograph to his youthful visitor, who deposited on the arm of his chair.

"I confess," he continued, "that it puzzles and disturbs me. It's preposterously archaeological, if you get what I mean. It isn't the sort of thing that one would—imagine."

Harris nodded. "I doubt if I could have imagined it from scratch. Without imaginative prompting or guidance from someone who had actually set eyes on it, it would be very difficult to conceive of anything so—so—"

"*Racial*," put in Doctor Imbert. "I believe that is the word you were groping for. That *thing* is a symbolic embodiment of the massed imaginative heritage of an entire people. It's a composite—like the Homeric epics or the Sphinx of Giza. It's the kind of art manifestation you would expect a primitive people to produce collectively. It's so perversely diabolical and contradictory in conception that one can scarcely conceive of a mere individual anywhere in the world deliberately sitting down and creating it out of his own imagination. I will concede that an unusually gifted artist might be *capable* of imagining it, but I doubt if such an obscenity would ever form in the human brain without a *raison d'être*. And no individual living in a civilized state would experience the need, the desire to imagine such a thing, and least of all, to give it objective expression.

"Mental illness, of course, might account for it, but the so-called interpretative reveries of psychotics are nearly always of predictable nature. Grotesque and absurd as they may sometimes be, certain images occur in them again and again and these images are definitely meaningful. They follow prescribed patterns, are crude and distorted representations of familiar objects and people. The morbidities out of which they arise have been studied and classified and a psychiatrist who knows his business can usually decipher them. If you have ever examined a batch of drawings from a mental institution you will have noticed how the same motifs occur repeatedly and how utterly *unimaginative* such things are from a sane and sophisticated point of view.

"It is of course true that the folk creations of primitive peoples usually embody or symbolize definite human preoccupations, but more boldly and imaginatively, and occasionally they depart from the predictable to such an extent that even our expert is obliged to throw up his hands.

"I have always believed that most of the major and minor monstrosities that figure so conspicuously in the pantheons of barbarian races—feathered serpents, animal-headed priests, grimacing sphinxes, etc., are synthetic conceptions. Let us suppose, for instance, that a tribe of reasonably enlightened barbarians is animated by the

55

unique social impulse of co-operative agriculture and is moved to embody its ideals in some colossal fetish designed to suggest both fertility and brotherhood—in, let us say, a great stone Magna Mater with arms outstretched to embrace all classes and conditions of men. Then let us suppose that co-operative agriculture falls into disrepute and the tribe becomes obsessed by dreams of martial conquest. What happens? To an obbligato of tomtoms and war drums the Mother Goddess is transfigured. A spear is placed between her extended arms, the expression of her face altered from benignity to ferocity, great gashes chiselled in her cheeks, red paint smeared on her arms, breasts and shoulders and her ears lopped off. Let another generation pass and the demoniac goddess of war will be transformed into something else—perhaps into a symbol of the most abandoned kind of debauchery.

"In a hundred years the original fetish will have become a monstrous caricature, a record in stone of the thoughts and emotions of generations of men.

"It is the business of the ethnologist and the archaeologist to decipher such records, and if our scientist is sufficiently learned and diligent he can, as you know, supply a reason for every peculiarity of configuration. Competent scholars have traced, in a rough way, the advance or retrogression of racial groups in ethical and aesthetic direction merely by studying and comparing their objects of worship and there does not exist a more fruitful science than idolography.

"But occasionally our ethnologist encounters a nut that he cannot crack, a god or goddess so diabolical or grotesque or loathsome in conformation that it is impossible to link it associatively with even the most revolting of tribal retrogressions. It is a notorious fact that human races are less apt to advance than circle back on the course of evolution, and that idols and fetishes that were originally conceived in a comparatively noble spirit very often become, in the course of time, embodiments of the bestial and the obscene. Some of the degraded objects of worship now employed by African bushmen and Australian aborigines may conceivably have been considerably less revolting ten or fifteen thousand years ago. It is impossible to predict the depths to which a race may descend and the appalling transformation which may occur in its 'sacred' imagery.

"And so occasionally we encounter shapes that we scarcely like to speculate about, shapes so *complicatedly* vile that they haven't even analogous counterparts in comparative mythology. Your fetish is of that nature. It is, as I say, preposterously archaeological and it differs unmistakably—although I am willing to concede a superficial resemblance—from the distorted dream images conjured up by psychotics and surrealistic artists. Only racial dissolution and decay extending over wide wastes of years could, in my opinion, account for such a ghastly anomaly."

He leaned forward and tapped Algernon significantly upon the knee. "You haven't told me its history," he admonished. "Reticence is an archaeologist's prerogative, and in our work it is always an asset, but for a young man you're almost abnormally addicted to it."

Algernon blushed to the roots of his hair. "I'm seldom actually reticent," he said. "At the Museum they all think I talk too much. I've an exuberant, officious way at times that positively appalls Mr. Scollard. But this affair is so—

so outside all normal experience that I've been dreading to tax your credulity with a résumé of it."

Doctor Imbert smiled. "Your books reveal that you are a very cautious and honest scholar," he said. "I don't believe I'd be inclined to question the veracity of whatever you may choose to tell me."

"Very well," said Algernon. "But I must entreat that you suspend judgement until you've heard all of the evidence. One can adduce rational explanations for each of the incidents I shall describe, but when one views them in the sequence in which they occurred they resolve themselves into a devastating hideous enigma."

Very tersely, without self-consciousness or affectation, Algernon then related all that he knew and all that he surmised and suspected that the thing whose image spread defilement on the paper before him.

Doctor Imbert heard him out in silence. But his eyes, as he listened, grew bright with horror.

"I doubt if I can help you," he said, when Algernon was done. "This thing transcends all of my experience."

There ensued a silence. Then Algernon said in a tone of desperate urgency, "But what *are* we to do? Surely you've something to suggest! "

Doctor Imbert rose shakingly to his feet. "I have—yes. I know someone who can, perhaps, help. He's a recluse, a psychic—a magnificent intellect obsessed by mysteries and mysticisms. I put little faith in such things—to me it's a degradation. But I'll take you to him. I'll take you anyway. God knows you're in trouble—that is obvious to me. And this man may be able to suggest something. Roger Little is his name. No doubt you've heard of him. He used to be a criminal investigator. A good one—a psychologist —discerning, erudite, shrewd—no mere detective-novel sleuth."

Algernon nodded understandingly. "Let us go to him at once," he said.

4. *The Horror on the Hills*

IT WAS WHILE Algernon and Doctor Imbert were journey-
ing in the subway toward Roger Little's residence in the
Borough of Queens that the Horror was announced to the
world. An account of its initial manifestation had been
flashed from Spain at midday to a great American news
syndicate and all of the New York papers had something
about it in their evening editions. The *News-Graphic's*
account was perhaps the most ominously disturbing in its
implications. A copywriter on that enterprising sheet had
surmised that the atrocities were distinguished by something outré, something altogether inexplicable, and by
choosing his diction with unusual care he had succeeded
in conveying to his unappreciative readers a tingling intimation of shockingness, of terror.

Beneath half-inch headlines which read: HIDEOUS
MASSACRE IN THE PYRENEES, he had written:

"The authorities are completely baffled. Who would wish
to assassinate fourteen simple peasants? They were found
at sundown on the mountain's crest. All in a row they lay,
very still, very pale—very silent and pale beneath the soft
Spanish sky. All about them stretched new-fallen snow

and beside them on the white expanse were marks, peculiar and baffling. Men do not make footprints a yard wide. And why were all the victims laid so evenly in a row? What violence was it that could deprive them of their heads, drain the blood from their bodies and lay them stark and naked in a row upon the snow?"

5. Little's Dream

"SOMEONE HAS BEEN MURDERED and so you wish my advice," murmured Roger Little wearily. "You wish the advice of a retired and eccentric recluse, well on in years, who has ceased to traffic with crime. I am quoting from a profile which did not appear in the *New Yorker*." He was staring into the fire and the bright radiance which streamed roomward from the grate so illumed the sharp outlines of his profile that Algernon was struck silent with awe.

"A positively Satanic presence," he murmured, to himself. "The exact facsimile of a sorcerer from the *Malleus Maleficarum*. They would have burned him in the Fifteenth Century."

"Murder," resumed Little, "has become a shabbily synthetic art and even the most daring masterpieces of the contemporary school are composed of inferior ingredients clumsily combined. Men no longer live in fear of the unknown, and that utter and abysmal disintegration of soul which the wise still call psychic evil no longer motivates our major atrocities. Anger, jealousy, and a paltry desire for material gain are pitiful emotional substitutes for the perverse and lonely egoism which inspired the great crimes of the Twelfth, Thirteenth and Fourteenth Centuries. When men killed with the deliberate certainty that they were jeopardizing their immortal souls and when the human body was regarded as a tabernacle for something more—or less—than human the crime of murder assumed epic and unholy proportions. The mere discovery of a mutilated cadaver in an age when men still believed in something—at least in *something*—filled every one with terror and with awe. Men, women and children took refuge behind barricaded doors and the more devout fell upon their knees, crossed themselves, lighted candles and chanted exorcisms.

"But in this decadent age when a human being is assassinated society merely shrugs its shoulders and relinquishes the sequel to the police. What have the police to do with a sacrament of evil in our midst? The sense of virtually immitigable evil, of stark unreasoning fear which murder once left in its wake, and the intense aesthetic enjoyment which certain individuals derived from merely studying such crimes as works of perverse and diabolical art have no parallels in contemporary experience. Hence it is that all modern murderers commit commonplace crimes—kill prosaically and almost indifferently without any suspicion that they are destroying more than lives of their unfortunate victims. And people go calmly about their business and are apparently not displeased to rub shoulders with the unholy ones in theatres, restaurants and subways!"

Algernon shifted excitedly in his chair. "But the problem we bring to you is enmeshed in the supernatural more hideously than any atrocity of the Ages of Faith. It transcends normal experience. If you will listen while I . . ."

Little shook his head. "I have written books—many books—describing dozens of instances of possession, of

63

return, of immolation, of divination, and of transformation. I have confirmed the reality of the *concubitus daemonum*; have proved incontestably the existence of vampires, succubi and lamias, and I have slipped not too unwillingly, into the warm and clinging arms of women five centuries dead."

He shuddered. "But what I have experienced in this very room is no more than a flickering shadow, swift-passing and obscurely glimpsed, of the horror that lurks Godlessly in undimensioned space. In my dreams I have heard the nauseous piping of its glutinous flutes and I have seen, terribly for an instant, the nets and trawls with which it angles for men."

"If you are convinced that such a horror exists . . ." Algernon began, but Little would not let him finish.

"My books have left most of my readers totally unconvinced, for it would disturb them to believe that I am not mentally unbalanced," he went on quickly.

"Erudite and brilliant, but as mad as Bruno when he was burned at the stake for refusing to keep his speculations about the nature of the physical universe to himself."

He rose passionately to his feet: "So I've definitely renounced the collection and correlation of facts," he said. "Hereafter I shall embody my unique convictions in the eloquent and persuasive guise of a fable. I shall write a novel. The art of fiction as a purveyor of essential truth has innumerable advantages which detached and impersonal utterance must of necessity lack. The fictioneer can familiarize his readers *gradually* with new and startling doctrines and avoid shocking them into a precipitous retreat into the shell of old and conventional beliefs. He can prevent them from succumbing to prejudice before they

64

have grasped one-quarter of the truths he is intent upon promulgating. Then, too, the artist can be so much more persuasive and eloquent than the scientist, and it can never be sufficiently emphasized that eloquence is never so effective in convincing men that certain things which are obviously false are momentarily true as it is in inducing them to discover that which is ultimately true beneath all the distortions of reality which can leave reason stranded in minds dominated by wishful thinking and a deep-seated fear of the unknown. Human wishes and desires are so eloquent in themselves that certainly some eloquence must be used in combating them. And that is why the mere scientist is so hopelessly at a loss when he seeks to convert others to what he himself believes to be the truth.

"He doesn't perceive that new truths must be presented to the human mind vividly, uniquely, as though one were initiating a mystery or instituting a sacrament, and that every failure to so present them decreases the likelihood that they will gain proponents, and that an entire civilization may pass away before any one arises with sufficient imagination and sufficient eloquence to take truths which have been enunciated once or twice coldly and forgotten because of the repugnance with which the common man regards fact barely recited and to clothe them in garments of terror and splendour and awe and so link them with far stars and the wind that moves above the water and the mystery and strangeness that will be in all things until the end of time."

Little's eyes were shining. "I have determined," he said, "to thrust aside the veil as fearlessly as Blake must have done when he wrote of a new heaven and a new earth, to fashion a garment so mind-beguiling in its beauty

65

that the ultimate revelation will remain cloaked until a spell has been cast which will permit of no drawing back, no craven surrender to fear."

He stopped suddenly, as if sobriety and an awareness of his surroundings had returned with a blood-rush to his entranced brain. "I have raved, no doubt. Like Blake, like Poe, like Gerard De Nerval I am always dreaming dreams, seeing visions. And to worldly men, calm and objective toward everyday realities, sceptical of all else, such visions, such glimpses are wholly incomprehensible. And you, no doubt, are inwardly pitying me and wondering how offended I would be if you should get up abruptly and plead a pressing engagement elsewhere. But if you only knew.

"There are things from *outside* watching always, secretly watching our little capers, our grotesque pranks. Men have disappeared. You're aware of that, aren't you? Men have disappeared within sight of their homes—at high noon, in the sunlight. Malignant and unknowable entities, *fishers* from outside have let down invisible tentacles, nets, trawls, and men and women have been caught up in a kind of pulsing darkness. A shadow seems to pass over them, to envelop them for an instant and then they are gone. And others have gone mad, witnessing such things.

"When a man ascends a flight of stairs it does not inevitably follow that he will arrive at the top. When a man crosses a street or a field or a public square it is not foreordained that he will reach the other side. *I have seen strange shadows in the sky.* Other worlds impinging on ours? I know that there are other worlds, but perhaps they do not *dimensionally* impinge. Perhaps from fourth,

66

fifth, six-dimensional worlds things with forms invisible to us, with faces veiled to us, reach down and take—instantaneously, mercilessly. Feeding on us perhaps? Using our brains for fodder? A few have glimpsed the truth for a terrifying instant in dreams. But it takes infinite patience and self-discipline, and years of study to establish waking contact, even for an instant, with the bodiless shapes that flicker appallingly in the void a thousand billion light years beyond the remotest of the spiral nebulae.

"Yet I—can do this. And you," he laughed, "come to me with a little mundane murder."

For an instant there was silence in the room. Then Algernon stood up, his face brightened by the flames that were still crackling in the grate. "You say," he exclaimed, "a little mundane murder. But to me it is more hideous, more alien to sanity and the world we know than all of your cosmic trawlers, and 'intrusions' from beyond."

Little shook his head. "No," he said. "I cannot believe that you are not exaggerating. It is so easy for men of exceptional intelligence to succumb at times to the fears, dreads, forebodings of ordinary men. Imaginative in a worldly sense, but blinder and dumber than clods cosmically. I am sure that I could unravel your puzzle with the most superficial layer of my waking mind, the little conscious mind that is so weak, so futile to grapple with anything more disturbing that what the body shall eat and drink and wear."

"If I had not seen," said Algernon, speaking very deliberately, "a stone thing shift its bulk, doing what the inanimate has never done in all the ages man has looked rationally upon it, I would have seriously doubted your sanity. It would be dishonest for me to pretend otherwise."

67

"A stone, you say, moved?" For the first time Little's interest quickened and a startled look came into his eyes.

"Yes, in the shape in which something—nature primeval perhaps, in eons primeval—shaped it. Moved in the night, unwatched by me. When Chaugnar Faugn . . ."

He stopped, was silent. For from his chair Little had sprung with a cry, his face bloodless, a cry of terror issuing from his thin lips.

"What is the matter?" gasped Doctor Imbert, and Algernon turned pale, not knowing what to make of so strange an occurrence. For Little seemed wholly undone, a mystic gone so completely mad that a violent outburst was only to be expected and might well be repeated, if he were not placed under immediate restraint. But at last he sank again into the chair from which he had so shockingly risen, and a trace of colour returned to his cheeks.

"Forgive me," he murmured brokenly. "Letting go like that was inexcusable. But when you mentioned Chaugnar Faugn I was for an instant mortally terrified."

He drew a deep breath. "The dream was so vivid that my mind rejected instantly a symbolic or allegorical interpretation. That name especially—Chaugnar Faugn. I was certain that something, somewhere, bore it—that the ghastliness that took Publius Libo on the high hills was an actuality, but not, I had hoped, an actuality for us. Something long past, surely, a horror of the ancient world that would never return to . . ." He broke off abruptly, seeming lost in thought.

"Tell me about it," he entreated, after a moment.

With bloodless lips Algernon related once again the history of Chaugnar Faugn as it had been related to him by Ulman, enhancing a little its hideousness by half-guesses and surmises of his own. Little listened in tight-lipped silence, his face a mask, only the throbbing of the veins on his temples betraying the agitation which wracked him. As Algernon concluded, the clock on the mantel, a tall, negro-coloured clock with wings on its shoulders and a great yellow ocean spider painted on its opalescent face, struck the hour: eleven even strokes pealed from it, shattering the stillness that had settled for an instant on the room. Algernon shivered, apprehensive at the lateness of the hour, fearful that in his absence Chaugnar Faugn might move again.

But now Little was speaking, striving painfully to keep his voice from sinking to a whisper.

"I had the dream last Halloween," he began, "and for detail, colour and sombre, brooding menace it surpasses anything of the kind I have experienced in recent years. It took form slowly, beginning as a nervous move from the atrium of my house into scroll-lined library to escape the sound of a fountain, and continuing as an earnest and friendly argument with a stout, firm-lipped man of about thirty-five, with strong, pure Roman features and the rather cumbersome equipment of a *legatus* in active military service. Impressions of identity and locale were so nebulous and gradual in their unfoldment as to be difficult to trace to a source, but they seem in retrospect to have been present from the first.

"The place was not Rome, nor even Italy, but the small provincial municipium of Calagurris on the south bank of the Iberus in Hispania Citerior. It was in the Republican age, because the province was still under a senatorial proconsul instead of a *legatus* of the Imperator. I was a

69

man of about my own waking age and build. I was clad in a civilian toga of yellowish colour with the two thin reddish stripes of the equestrian order. My name was L. Caelius Rufus and my rank seemed to be that of a provincial quaestor. I was definitely an Italian-born Roman, the province of Calagurris being alien, colonial soil to me. My guest was Cnaeus Balbitius, *legatus* of the XII Legion, which was permanently encamped just outside the town on the riverbank. The home in which I was receiving him was a suburban villa on a hillside south of the compact section, and it overlooked both town and river.

"The day before I had received a worried call from one Tib. Annaeus Mela, edile of the small town of Pompelo, three days' march to the north in the territory of the Vascones at the foot of the mysterious Pyrenees. He had been to request Balbutius to spare him a cohort for a very extraordinary service on the night of the Kalends of November and Balbutius had emphatically refused. Therefore, knowing me to be acquainted with P. Scribonius Libo, the proconsul at Tarraco, he had come to ask me to lay his case by letter before that official. Mela was a dark, lean man of middle age, of presentable Roman features but with the coarse hair of a Celtiberian.

"It seems that there dwelt hidden in the Pyrenees a strange race of small dark people unlike the Gauls and Celtiberians in speech and features, who indulged in terrible rites and practices twice every year, on the Kalends of Maius and November. They lit fires on the hilltops at dusk, beat continuously on strange drums and horribly all through the night. Always before these orgies people would be found missing from the village and none of them were ever known to return. It was thought that they were

70

stolen for sacrificial purposes, but no one dared to investigate, and eventually the semi-annual loss of villagers came to be regarded as a regular tribute, like the seven youths and maidens that Athens was forced to send each year to Crete for King Minos and the Minotaur.

"The tribal Vascones and even some of the semi-Romanized cottages of the foothills were suspected by the inhabitants of Pompelo of being in league with the strange dark folk—*Miri Nigri* was the name used in my dream. These dark folk were seen in Pompelo only once a year—in summer, when a few of their number would come down from the hills to trade with the merchants. They seemed incapable of speech and transacted business by signs.

"During the preceding summer the small folk had come to trade as usual—five of them—but had become involved in a general scuffle when one of them had attempted to torture a dog for pleasure in the forum. In this fighting two of them had been killed and the remaining three had returned to the hills with evil faces. Now it was autumn and *the customary quota of villagers had not disappeared.* It was not normal for the Miri Nigri thus to spare Pompelo. Clearly they must have reserved the town for some terrible doom, which they would call down on their unholy sabbath night as they drummed and howled and danced outrageously on the mountain's crest. Fear walked through Pompelo and the edile Mela had come to Calagurris to ask for a cohort to invade the hills on the sabbath night and break up the obscene rites before the ceremony might be brought to a head. But Balbutius had laughed at him and refused. He thought it poor policy for the Roman administration to meddle in local quarrels. So Mela had been obliged to come to me. I enheartened him as best I could, and

71

promised help, and he returned to Pompelo at least partly reassured.

"Before writing the proconsul I had thought it best to argue with Balbutius himself, so I had been to see him at the camp, found him out and left word with a centurion that I would welcome a call from him. Now he was here and reiterated his belief that we ought not to complicate our administration by arousing the resentment of the tribesmen, as we undoubtedly would if we attempted to suppress a rite with which they were obviously in ill-concealed sympathy.

"I seemed to have read considerable about the dark rites of certain unknown and wholly barbaric races, for I recall feeling a sense of monstrous impending doom and trying my best to induce Balbutius to put down the sabbath. To his objections I replied that it had never been the custom of the Roman people to be swayed by the whims of the barbarians when the fortunes of Roman citizens were in danger and that he ought not to forget the status of Pompelo as a legal colony, small as it was. That the good-will of the tribal Vascones was little to be depended upon at best, and that the trust and friendship of the Romanized townsfolk, in whom was more than a little of our own blood after three generations of colonization, was a matter of far greater importance to the smooth work-ing of that provincial government on which the security of the Roman imperium primarily rested. Furthermore, that I had reason to believe, from my studies, that the appre-hensions of the Pompelonians were disturbingly well-founded, and that there was indeed brewing in the high hills a monstrous doom which it would ill become the traditions of Rome to countenance. That I would be

72

surprised to encounter laxity in the representatives of those whose ancestors had not hesitated to put to death large numbers of Roman citizens for participation in the orgies of Bacchus and had ordered engraved on public tablets of bronze the *Senatus Consultum de Bacchanalibus.*

"But I could not influence Balbutius. He went away courteously but unmoved. So I at once took a reed pen and wrote a letter to the proconsul Libo, sealing it and calling for a wiry young slave—a Greek called Antipater— to take it to Tarraco.

"The following morning I went out on foot, down the hill to the town and through the narrow block-paved streets with high white-washed dead-walls and gaudily painted shops with awnings. The crowds were very vivid. Legionaries of all races, Roman colonists, tribal Celtiberi, Romanized natives, Romanized and Iberized Cathaginians, mongrels of all sorts. I spoke to only one person, a Roman named Aebutius, about whom I recall nothing. I visited the camp—a great area with an earthen wall ten feet high and streets of wooden huts inside, and I called at the *praetorium* to tell Balbutius that I had written the proconsul. He was still pleasant but unmoved. Later I went home, read in the garden, bathed, dined, talked with the family and went to bed—having, a little later, a nightmare *within the dream* which centred about a dark terrible desert with cyclopean ruins of stones and a malign presence over all.

"About noon the next day—I had been reading in the garden—the Greek returned with a letter and enclosure from Libo. I broke the seal and read: 'P. SCRIBONIVS L. CAELIO. S. D. SI. TV. VALES. VALEO. QVAE SCRIPSISTI. AVDIVI. NEC. ALIAS, PVTO.'

"In a word, the proconsul agreed with me—had known about the Miri Nigri himself—and enclosed an order for the advance of the cohort to Pompelo at once, by forced marches, in order to reach the doom-shadowed town on the day before the fatal Kalends. He requested me to accompany it because of my knowledge of what the mysterious rites were whispered to be, and furthermore declared his design of going along himself, saying that he was even then on the point of setting out and would be in Pompelo before we could be.

"I lost not a second in going personally to the camp and handing the orders to Balbutius, and I must say he took his defeat gracefully. He decided to send Cohors V, under Sextus Asellius, and presently summoned that *legatus*—a slim, supercilious youth with frizzed hair and a fashionable fringe of beard-growth on his under jaw. Asellius was openly hostile to the move but dared not disregard orders. Balbutius said he would have the cohort at the bridge across the Iberus in an hour and I rushed home to prepare for the rough day and night march.

"I put on a heavy paenula and ordered a litter with six Illyrian bearers, and reached the bridge ahead of the cohort. At last, though, I saw the silver eagles flashing along the street to my left, and Balbutius—who had decided at the last moment to go along himself—rode out ahead and accompanied my litter ahead of the troops as we crossed the bridge and struck out over the plains toward the mystic line of dimly glimpsed violet hills. There was no long sleep during all the march, but we had naps and brief halts and bites of lunch—cakes and cheese. Balbutius usually rode by my litter in conversation (it was infantry, but he and Asellius were mounted) but sometimes I read—

M. Porcius Cato *De Re Rustica,* and a hideous manuscript in Greek, which made me shudder even to touch or look at but of which I cannot remember a single word.

"The second morning we reached the whitewashed houses of Pompelo and trembled at the fear that was on the place. There was a wooden amphitheatre east of the village, and a large open plain on the west. All the immediate ground was flat, but the Pyrenees rose up green and menacing on the north, looking nearer than they were. Scribonius Libo had reached there ahead of us with his secretary, Q. Trebellius Pollio, and he and the edile Mela greeted us in the forum. We all—Libo, Pollio, Mela, Balbutius, Asellius and I—went into the curia (an excellent new building with a Corinthian portico) and discussed ways and means, and I saw that the proconsul was with me heart and soul.

"But Balbutius and Asellius continued to argue and at times the discussion grew very tense. Libo was an utterly admirable old man, and he insisted on going into the hills with the rest of us and seeing the awful revelations of the night. Mela, ghastly with fright, promised horses to those of us who were not mounted. He had pluck—for he meant to go himself.

"It is impossible even to suggest the stark and ghastly terror which hung over this phase of the dream.

"Surely there never was such evil as that which brooded over the accursed town as the sinking sun threw long menacing shadows amidst the reddening afternoon. The legionaires fancied they heard the rustling of stealthy, unseen and ominously deliberate presences in the black encircling woods. Occasionally a torch had to be lighted

75

momentarily in order to keep the frightened three hundred together, but for the most part it was a dreadful scramble through the dark. A slit of northern sky was visible ahead between the terrible, cliff-like slopes that encompassed us and I marked the chair of Cassiopeia and the golden powder of the Via Lactea. Far, far ahead and above and appearing to merge imperceptibly into the heavens, the lines of remoter peaks could be discerned, each capped by a sickly point of unholy flame. And still the distant, hellish drums pounded incessantly on.

"At length the route grew too steep for the horses and the six of us who were mounted were forced to take to our feet. We left the horses tethered to a clump of scrub oaks and stationed ten men to guard them, though heaven knows it was no night nor place for petty thieves to be abroad! And then we scrambled on—jostling, stumbling and sometimes climbing with our hands' help up places little short of perpendicular. Suddenly a sound behind us made every man pause as if hit by an arrow. It was from the horses we had left, and it did not cease. They were not neighing but *screaming*. They were screaming, mad with some terror beyond any this earth knows. No sound came up from the men we had left with them. Still they screamed on, and the soldiers around us stood trembling and whimpering and muttering fragments of a prayer to Rome's gods, and the gods of the East and the gods of the barbarians.

"Then there came a sharp scuffle and yell from the front of the column which made Asellius call quaveringly for a torch. There was a prostrate figure weltering in a growing and glistening pool of blood and we saw by the faint flare that it was the young guide Accius. He had killed himself because of the sound he had heard. He, who had been born and bred at the foot of those terrible hills and had heard dark whispers of their secrets, knew well why the horses had screamed. And because he knew, he had snatched a sword from the scabbard of the nearest soldier —the centurion P. Vibulanus—and had plunged it full-length into his own breast.

"At this point pandemonium broke loose because of something noticed by such of the men as were able to notice anything at all. *The sky had been snuffed out.* No longer did Cassiopeia and Via Lactea glimmer betwixt the hills, but stark blackness loomed behind the continuously swelling fires on the distant peaks. And still the horses screamed and the far-off drums pounded hideously and incessantly on.

"Cackling laughter broke out in the black woods of the vertical slopes that hemmed us in and around the swollen fires of the distant peaks we saw prancing and leaping the awful and cyclopean silhouettes of things that were neither men nor beasts, but fiendish amalgams of both—things with huge flaring ears and long waving trunks that howled and gibbered and pranced in the skyless night. And a cold wind coiled purposively down from the empty abyss, winding sinuously about us till we started in fresh panic and struggled like Laocoon and his sons in the serpent's grasp.

"There were terrible sights in the light of the few shaking torches. Legionaires trampled one another to death and screamed more hoarsely than the horses far below. Of our immediate party Trebellius Pollio had long vanished, and I saw Mela go down beneath the heavy caligae of a gigantic Aquitanian. Balbutius had gone mad

77

and was grinning and simpering out an old Fescennine verse recalled from the Latin countryside of his boyhood. Asellius tried to cut his own throat, but the sentient wind held him powerless, so that he could do nothing but scream and scream and scream above the cackling laughter and the screaming horses and the distant drums and the howling colossal shapes that capered about the demon-fires on the peaks.

"I myself was frozen to the helplessness of a statue and could not move or speak. Only old Publius Libo the proconsul was strong enough to face it like a Roman— Publius Scribonius Libo, who had gone through the Jugurthine and Mithridatic and social wars—Publius Libo three times praetor and three times consul of the republic, in whose atrium stood the ancestral forms of a hundred heroes. He and he alone had the voice of a man and of a general and triumphator. I can see him now in the dimming light of those horrible torches, among that fear-struck stampede of the doomed. I can hear him still as he spoke his last words, gathering up his toga with the dignity of a Roman and a consul: *'Malitia vetus—malitia vetus est— venit—tandem venit . . .'*

"And then the wooded encircling slopes burst forth with louder cackles and I saw that they were slowly moving. The hills—the terrible living hills—were closing up upon their prey. The Miri Nigri had called their terrible gods out of the void.

"Able to shriek at last, I awoke in a sea of cold perspiration.

"Calagurris, as you probably know, is a real and well-known town of Roman Spain, famed as the birthplace of

78

the rhetorician Quintilianus. Upon consulting a classical dictionary I found Pompelo also to be real. and surviving today as the Pyrenean village of Pampelona."

He ceased speaking, and for a moment the three men were silent. Then Algernoon said: "The Chinaman had a strange dream too. He spoke of the horror on the mountains —of great things that came clumping down from the hills at nightfall."

Little nodded. "Mongolians as a rule are extremely psychic," he said. "I have known several whose clairvoyant gifts were superior to a yoga adept's often astounding feats of precognition."

"And you think that Hsieh Ho's dream was a prophecy?" whispered Imbert.

"I do. Some monstrous *unfettering* is about to take place. That which for two thousand years has lain somnolent will stir again and the 'great things' will descend from their frightful lair on the Spanish hills drawn cityward through the will of Chaugnar Faugn. We are in propinquity to the primal, hidden horror that festers at the root of being, with the old, hidden loathsomeness which Greeks and Romans veiled under the symbolic form of a man-beast—*the feeder, the all*. The Greeks knew, for the horror left its lair to ravage, striding eastward in the dawn across Europe, wading waist-deep in the dark Ionian seas, looming monstrous at nightfall over Delos, and Samothrace and far-off Crete. A nimbus of starfoam engirdled its waist; suns, constellations gleamed in its eyes. But its breath brought madness, and its embrace, death. The feeder—the all."

The telephone bell at Little's elbow was jangling disconcertingly. Stretching forth a tremulous hand he grasped the receiver firmly and laid it against his cheek. "Hello," he whispered into the mouthpiece. "What is it? Who is speaking?"

"From the Manhattan Museum." The words smote ominously upon his ear. "Is Mr. Algernon Harris there? I phoned Doctor Imbert's house and they gave me this number."

"Yes, Harris is here." Little's voice was vibrant with apprehension. "I'll call him."

He turned the instrument over to Algernon and sank back exhaustedly in his chair. For a moment the latter conversed in a low tone; then an expression of stunned incredulity appeared on his face. His hand shook as he put back the receiver and tottered toward the fireplace. For an instant he stood staring intensely into the coals, his fingers gripping the mantel's edge so tightly that his knuckles showed white. When he turned there was a look of utter consternation in his eyes.

"Chaugnar Faugn has disappeared," he cried. "Chaugnar Faugn has left the museum. No one saw him go and the idiot who phoned thinks that a thief removed him. Or possibly one of the attendants. But *we* know how unlikely that is."

"I'm afraid we do," Little said, grimly. "I am to blame," Algernon went on quickly. "I should have insisted they patrol the alcove. I should have at least explained to them that someone might try to steal Chaugnar Faugn, even if Ulman's story had to be kept from them."

He shook his head in helpless frustration.

"No . . . no . . . that would have done no good. A watchman would have been utterly impotent to cope with such a horror. Chaugnar Faugn would have destroyed him hide-ously in an instant. And now it is loose in the streets!"

He walked to the window and stared across the glittering harbour at the darkly looming skyline of lower Manhattan. "It is loose over there," he cried, raising his arm and point-ing. "It is crouching in the shadows somewhere, alert and waiting, preparing to . . ." He broke off abruptly, as if the vision his mind had conjured up was too ghastly to dwell upon.

Little rose and laid a steadying hand on Algernon's arm. "I haven't said I couldn't help," he said. "Though Chaugnar Faugn is a very terrible menace it isn't quite as omnipotent as Ulman thought. It and its brothers are incarnate manifestations of a very ancient, a very malignant hyperdimensional entity. Or call it a principle, if you wish —a principle so antagonistic to life as we know it that it becomes a spreading blight, as destructive as a nest of cancer cells would be if cancer could be transplanted by surgical means into healthy tissue, and continue to grow and proliferate until every vestige of healthy tissue has been destroyed. But it is a cancer whose growth I can at least retard. And if I am successful I can send it back to its point of origin beyond the galactic universe, can cut it asunder forever from our three-dimensional world. Had I known that the horror still lurked in the Pyrenees I should have gone, months ago, to *send* it back. Yes, even though the thought of it now fills me with a loathing un-speakable, I should have gone.

"I am not," he continued, "a merely theoretical dreamer. Though I am by temperament disposed toward specula-tions of a mystical nature, I have forged a very concrete and effective weapon to combat the cosmic malignancies.

If you'll step into my laboratory I'll show you something which should restore your confidence in the experimental capacity of the human mind when there is but one choice confronting it—to survive or go down forever into everlasting night and darkness."

6. *The Time-Space Machine*

ROGER LITTLE'S LABORATORY was illumed by a single bluish lamp embedded in the concrete of its sunken floor. An infinite diversity of mechanism lined the walls and sprawled their precise lengths on long tables and dangled eerily from hooks set in the high, domed ceiling; mechanisms a-glitter in blue-lit seclusion, a strange, bizarre fore-glimpse into the alchemy and magic of a far-distant future, with spheres and condensers and gleaming metal rods in lieu of stuffed crocodiles and steaming elixirs.

All of the contrivances were arresting, but one was so extraordinary in size and complexity that it dominated the others and riveted Algernon's attention. He seemed unable to drag his gaze from the thing. It was a strange agglomeration of metallic spheres and portions of spheres, of great bluish globes surrounded by tiny clusters of half globes and quarter-globes, whose surfaces converged in a most fantastic way. And from the globes there sprouted at grotesque angles metallic crescents with converging tips.

To Algernon's excited imagination the thing wore a quasi-reptilian aspect. "It's like a toad's face," he muttered. "Bulbous and bestial."

Little nodded. "It's a triumph of mechanical ugliness, isn't it? Yet it would have been deified in Ancient Greece— by Archimedes especially. He would have exalted it above all his Conoids and Parabolas."

"What function does it perform?" asked Algernon.

"A sublime one. It's a time-space machine. But I'd rather not discuss its precise function until I've shown you how it works. I want you to study its face as it waxes non-Euclidean. When you've glimpsed a fourth-dimensional figure you'll be prepared to concede, I think, that the claims I make for it are not extravagant. I know of no more certain corrective for an excess of scepticism. I was the *Critique of Pure Reason* personified until I looked upon a *skinned sphere*—then I grew very humble, reverent toward the great *Suspected*.

"Watch now." He reached forward, grasped a switch and with a swift downward movement of his right arm set the machine in motion. At first the small spheres and the crescents revolved quickly and the large spheres slowly; then the large spheres literally spun while the small spheres lazed, and then both small spheres and large spheres moved in unison. Then the spheres stopped altogether, but only for an instant, while something of movement seemed to flow into them from the revolving crescents. Then the crescents stopped and the spheres moved, in varying tempo, faster and faster, and their movement seemed to flow back into the crescents. Then both crescents and spheres began to move in unison, faster and faster and faster, until the entire mass seemed to merge into a shape paradoxical, outrageous, unthinkable—a spheroid with a non-Euclidean face, a geometric blasphemy that was at once isosceles and equilateral, convex and concave.

84

Algernon stared in horror. "What in God's name is that?" he cried.

"You are looking on a fourth-dimensional figure," said Little soothingly. "Steady now."

For an instant nothing happened; then a light, greenish, blinding, shot from the centre of the crazily distorted figure and streamed across the opposite wall, limning on the smooth cement a perfect circle.

But only for a second was the wall illumed. With an abrupt movement Little shot the lever upward and its radiance dimmed, and vanished. "Another moment, and that wall would have crumbled away," he said.

With fascination Algernon watched the outrageous spheroid grow indistinct, watched it blur and disappear amidst a resurgence of spheres.

"That light," cried Little exultantly, "will send Chaugnar Faugn back through time. It will reverse its decadent *randomness*—disincarnate and disembody it, and send it back forever."

"But I don't understand," murmured Algernon. "What do you mean by *randomness*."

"I mean that this machine can work havoc with entropy!" There was a ring of exaltation in Little's voice.

"Entropy?" Algernon scowled. "I'm not sure that I understand. I know what entropy *is* in thermodynamics, of course, but I'm not sure . . ."

"I'll explain," said Little. "You are of course familiar with the A B C's of Einsteinian physics and are aware that time is *relatively* arrowless, that the sequence in which we view events in nature is not a cosmic actuality and that our conviction that we are going somewhere in time is a purely human illusion conditioned by our existence

85

on this particular planet and the limitations which our five senses impose upon us. We divide time into past, present and future, but in reality an event's sequence in time depends wholly on the position in space from which it is viewed. Events which occurred thousands of years ago on this planet haven't as yet taken place to a hypothetical observer situated billions and billions of light years remote from us. Thus, cosmically speaking, we can not say of an event that it has happened and will never happen again or that it is about to happen and has never happened before, because 'before' to us is 'after' to intelligences situated elsewhere in space and time.

    "But though our familiar time-divisions are purely arbitrary there is omnipresent in nature a principle called entropy which, as Eddington has pointed out, equips time with a kind of empirical arrow. The entire universe appears to be 'running down.' It is the consensus of astronomical opinion that suns and planets and electrons are constantly breaking up, becoming more and more *disorganized*. Billions of years ago some mysterious dynamic, which Sir James Jeans has likened to the Finger of God, streamed across primeval space and created the universe of stars in a state of almost perfect integration, welded them into a system so highly organized that there was only the tiniest manifestation of the random element anywhere in it. The random element in nature is the uncertain element—the principle which brings about disorganizations, disintegration, decay.

    "Let us suppose that two mechanical men, robots, are tossing a small ball to and fro, to and fro. The process may go on indefinitely, for the mechanical creatures do not tire and there is nothing to make the ball swerve from.

its course. But now let us suppose that a bird in flight collides with the ball, sends it spinning so that it misses the hand of the receiving robot. What happens? Both robots begin to behave grotesquely. Missing the ball, their arms sweep through the empty air, making wider and wider curves and they stagger forward perhaps, and collapse in each other's arms. The random, the uncertain element has entered their organized cosmos and they have ceased to function.

"This tendency of the complex to disintegrate, of the perfectly-balanced to run amuck, is called entropy. It is entropy that provides time with an arrow and, disrupting nebulae, plays midwife to the birth of planets from star-wombs incalculable. It is entropy that cools great orbs, hotter than Betelgeuse, more fiery than Arcturus through all the outer vastness, reducing them to sterility, to whirling motes of chaos.

"It is the random element that is slowly breaking up, destroying the universe of stars. In an ever widening circle, with an ever increasing malignancy—if one may ascribe malignancy to a force, a tendency—it works its awful havoc. It is analogous to a grain of sand dropped into one of the interstices of a vast and intricate machine. The grain creates a small disturbance which in turn creates a larger one, and so on ad infinitum.

"And with every event that has occurred on this earth since its departure from the sun there has been an increase of the random element. Thus we can legitimately 'place' events in time. Events which occurred ten of thousands of years ago may be happening now to intelligences situated elsewhere, and events still in the offing, so to speak, may exist already in another dimension of space-time. But if an earth-event is very disorganized and very decadent in its contours even our hypothetical distant observer would know that it has occurred very late in the course of cosmic evolution and that a series of happier events, with less of the random element in them, must have preceded it in time. In brief, that sense of time's passing which we experience in our daily lives is due to our intuitive perception that the structure of the universe is continuously breaking down. Every thing that 'happens,' every event, is an objective manifestation of matter's continuous and all-persuasive decay and disintegration."

Algernon nodded. "I think I understand. But doesn't that negate all that we have been taught to associate with the word 'evolution'? It means that not advancement but an *inherent* degeneration has characterized all the processes of nature from the beginning of time. Can we apply it to man? Do you mean to suggest . . ."

Little shrugged. "One can only speculate. It may be that mediaeval theology wasn't so very wrong after all—that old Augustine and the Angelic Doctor and Abelard and the others surmised correctly, that man was once akin to the angels and that he joined himself to nature's decay through a deliberate rejection of heaven's grace. It may be that by some mysterious and incomprehensibly perverse act of will he turned his face from his Maker and let evil pour in upon him, made of himself a magnet for all the malevolence that the cosmos holds. There may have been more than a little truth in Ulman's identification of Chaugnar with the Lucifer of mediaeval myth."

"Is this," exclaimed Imbert, reproachfully, "a proper occasion for a discussion of theology?"

"It isn't," Little acknowledged. "But I thought it desir-

88

able to outline certain—possibilities. I don't want you to imagine that I regard the intrusion of Chaugnar Faugn into our world as a scientifically explicable occurrence in a facilely dogmatic sense."

"I don't care how you regard it," affirmed Algernon, "so long as you succeed in destroying it utterly. I am a profound agnostic as far as religious concepts are concerned. But the universe is mysterious enough to justify divergent speculations on the part of intelligent men as to the ultimate nature of reality."

"I quite agree," Little said. "I was merely pointing out that modern science alone has very definite limitations."

"And yet you propose to combat this . . . this horror with science," exclaimed Imbert.

"With a concrete embodiment of the concepts of transcendental mathematics," corrected Little. "And such concepts are merely empirically scientific. I am aware that science may be loosely defined as a systematized accumulation of tendencies and principles, but classically speaking, its prime function is to convey some idea of the nature of reality by means of an inductive logic. Yet our mathematical physicist has turned his face from induction as resolutely as did the mediaeval scholastics in the days of the Troubadours. He insists that we must start from the universal assumption that we can never know positively the real nature of anything, and that whatever 'truth' we may deduce from empirical generalities will be chiefly valuable as a kind of mystical guidepost, at best merely roughly indicative of the direction in which we are travelling; but withal, something of a sacrament and therefore superior to the dogmatic 'knowledge' of Nineteenth Century science. The speculations of mathematical physicists today are more like poems and psalms than anything else. They embody concepts wilder and more fantastic than anything in Poe or Hawthorne or Blake."

He stepped forward and seized the entropy-reversing machine by its globular neck. "Two men can carry it very easily," he said, as he lifted it a foot from the floor by way of experiment. "We can train it on Chaugnar Faugn from a car."

"If it keeps to the open streets," interjected Algernon. "We can't follow it up a fire-escape or into the woods in a car."

"I'd thought of that. It could hide itself for days in Central Park or Inwood or Van Cortland Park or the wider stretches of woodland a little further to the north but still close to the city. But we won't cross that bridge until we come to it." His expression was tense, but he spoke with quiet deliberation. "We could dispense with the car in an emergency," he said. "Two men could advance fairly rapidly with the machine on a smooth expanse."

"We must make haste," he continued, after a moment. "It's my chauffeur's day off, but I'll take a taxi down to the garage and get the car myself." He turned to Algernon. "If you want to help, locate Chaugnar Faugn."

Algernon stared. "But how . . ." he gasped.

"It shouldn't be difficult. Get in touch with the police—Assistance and Ambulance Division. Ask if they've received any unusually urgent calls, anything of a sensational nature. If Chaugnar has slain again they'll know about it."

He pointed urgently toward a phone in the corner and strode from the laboratory.

7. A Cure for Scepticism

WHEN ALGERNON had completed his phone call he lit a cigarette very calmly and deliberately and crossed to where Doctor Imbert was standing. Only the trembling of his lower lip betrayed the agitation he was having difficulty in controlling. "There have been five emergency calls," he said, "all from the midtown section—between Thirty-fifth and Forty-eighth Streets."

Imbert grew pale. "And—and deaths?"

Algernon nodded. "And deaths. Two of the ambulances have just returned."

"How many were killed?"

"They don't know yet. There were five bodies in the first ambulance—three men, a woman and a little girl—a negress. All horribly mutilated. They've gone wild over there. The chap who spoke to me wanted to know what I knew, why I had phoned—he shouted at me, broke down and sobbed."

"God!"

"There's nothing we can do till Little gets back," Algernon said.

"And then? What do you suppose we can do then?"

"The machine . . ." Algernon began and stopped. He couldn't endure putting the way he felt about Little's machine, and the doubts he had entertained concerning it into words. It was necessary to believe in the machine, to have confidence in Little's sagacity—supreme confidence. It would have been disastrous to doubt in such a moment that a blow would eventually be struck, that Little and his machine together would dispose, forever, of the ghastly menace of Chaugnar Faugn. But to defend such a faith rationally, to speak boldly and with confidence of a mere intuitive conviction was another matter.

"You know perfectly well that Little's mentally unbalanced," affirmed Imbert, "that it would be madness to credit his assertions." He gestured toward the machine. "That thing is merely a mechanical hypnotizer. Ingenious, I concede—it can induce twilight sleep with a rapidity I wouldn't have thought possible—but it is quite definitely three-dimensional. It brings the subconscious to the fore, the subconscious that believes everything it is told, induces temporary somnolence while Little whispers: 'You are gazing on a fourth-dimensional figure. You are gazing on a fourth-dimensional figure.' Such deceptions aren't difficult to implant when the mind is in a dreamlike state."

"I'd rather not discuss it," murmured Algernon. "I can't believe the figure we saw was wholly a deception. It was too ghastly and unbelievable. And remember that we both saw the same figure. I was watching you at the time—you looked positively ill. And mass hypnotism is virtually an impossibility. You ought to know that. No two men will respond to suggestion in the same way. We *both* saw a four-dimensional figure—an outrageous figure."

"But how do you know we both saw the same figure?

We may easily have responded differently to Little's suggestion. Group hypnotism is possible in that sense. I saw something decidedly disturbing and so did you, but that doesn't prove that we weren't hypnotized."

"I'll convince you that we weren't," exclaimed Algernon. "A time-space machine of this nature isn't theoretically inconceivable, for physicists have speculated on the possibility of reversing entropy in isolated portions of matter for years. Watch now! "

Deliberately he walked to the machine and shot the lever upward.

8. *What Happened in the Laboratory*

ALGERNON RAISED HIMSELF on his elbow and stared in horror at the gaping hole in the wall before him. It was a great circular hole with jagged edges and through it the sky-line of lower Manhattan glimmered nebulously, like an etching under glass. His temples throbbed painfully; his tongue was dry and swollen and adhered to the roof of his mouth.

Some one was standing above him. Not Imbert, for Imbert wore spectacles. And this man's face was destitute of glitter, a blurred oval faultlessly white. Confusedly Algernon recalled that Little did not wear spectacles. This, then, was Little. Little, not Imbert. It was coming back now. He had sought to convince Imbert that the machine wasn't a mechanical hypnotizer. He had turned it on and then—Good God! what had happened then? Something neither of them had anticipated. An explosion! But first for an instant they had seen the figure. And the light. And he and Imbert had been too frightened—too frightened to turn it off. How very clear it was all becoming. They had stood for an instant facing the wall, too utterly bewildered

94

to turn off the light. And then Little had entered the room, and he had shouted a warning—a frenzied warning.

"Help me, please," exclaimed Algernon weakly.

Little bent and gripped him by the shoulders. "Steady, now," he commanded, as he guided him toward a chair. "You're not hurt. You'll be all right in a moment. Imbert, too, is all right. A piece of plaster struck him in the temple, gave him a nasty cut, but he'll be quite all right."

"But—what happened?" Algernon gestured helplessly toward the hole in the wall. "I remember that there was an explosion and that—you shouted at me, didn't you?"

"Yes, I shouted for you to get back into the room. You were standing too close to the wall. Another instant and the floor would have crumbled too and you'd have had a nasty tumble—a tumble from which you wouldn't have recovered."

He smiled grimly and patted Algernon on the shoulder. "Just try to calm down a bit. I'll get you a whisky and soda."

"But what, precisely happened?" persisted Algernon.

"The light decreased the wall's *randomness*, sent it back through time. I warned you that the wall would crumble if the light rested on it for more than an instant. But you had to experiment."

"I'm sorry," muttered Algernon shamefacedly. "I fear I've ruined your apartment."

"Not important, really. It's eery, of course, having all one's secrets open to the sky, but my landlord will rectify that." He gazed at Algernon curiously. "Why did you do it?" he asked.

"To convince Imbert. He said the machine was merely a mechanical hypnotizer."

"I see, Imbert thought I was rather pathetically 'touched'."

"Not exactly. I think he wanted to believe you . . ."

"But couldn't. Well, I can't blame him. Five years ago I would have doubted too—laughed all this to scorn. I approve of sceptics. They're dependable—when you've succeeded in convincing them that unthinkable and outrageous things occasionally have at least a pragmatic potency. I doubt if even now Imbert would concede that this is an entropy-reversing machine, but you may be sure his respect for it has grown. He'll follow my instructions now without hesitation. And I want you to. We must act in unison, or we'll be defeated before we start."

Algernon began suddenly to tremble. "We haven't an instant to lose," he exclaimed. "I got in touch with the police just before you came back—they're sending out ambulance calls from all over the city. Chaugnar has begun to slay—" Algernon had risen and was striding toward the door.

"Wait! " Little's voice held a note of command. "We've got to wait for Imbert. He's downstairs in the bathroom dressing his wound."

Reluctantly Algernon returned into the room.

"A few minutes' delay won't matter," continued Little, his voice surprisingly calm. "We've such a hideous ordeal before us that we should be grateful for this respite."

"But Chaugnar is killing now," protested Algernon. "And we are sitting here letting more lives . . ."

"Be snuffed out? Perhaps. But at the same instant all over the world other lives are being snuffed out by diseases which men could prevent if they energetically bestirred themselves." He drew a deep breath. "We're doing the best we can, man. This respite is necessary for our nerves' sake. Try to view the situation sanely. If we are going to eradicate the malignancy which is Chaugnar Faugn we'll need a surgeon's calm. We've got to steel our wills, extrude from our minds all hysterical considerations, and all sentiment."

"But it will kill thousands," protested Algernon. "In the streets . . ."

"No." Little shook his head. "It's no longer in the streets. It has left the city."

"How do you know know?"

"There has been a massacre on the Jersey coast—near Asbury Park. I stopped for an instant in the *Brooklyn Standard* office on my way up from the garage. The night staff's in turmoil. They're rushing through a sensational morning extra. I found out something else. There's been a similar massacre in Spain! If we hadn't been talking here we'd have known. All the papers ran columns about it—hours ago. They're correlating the dispatches now and by tomorrow every one will know of the menace. What I fear is mass hysteria."

"Mass hysteria?"

"Yes, they'll go mad in the city tomorrow—there'll be a stampede. Unreasoning superstition and blind terror always culminate in acts of violence. Hundreds of people will run amuck, pillage, destroy. There'll be more lives lost than Chaugnar destroyed tonight."

"But we can do something. We must."

"I said that we were merely waiting for Doctor Imbert." Little crossed to the eastern window and stared for a moment into the lightening sky. Then he returned to where Algernon was standing. "Do you feel better?" he asked. "Have you pulled yourself together?"

"Yes," muttered Algernon. "I'm quite all right."

"Good."

The door opened and Imbert came in. His face was distraught and of a deathly pallor, but a look of relief came into his eyes when they rested on Algernon. "I feared you were seriously hurt," he cried. "We were quite mad to experiment with—with that thing."

"We must experiment again, I fear."

Imbert nodded. "I'm ready to join you. What do you want us to do?"

"I want you and Harris to carry that machine downstairs and put it into my car. I'll need a flashlight and a few other things. I won't be long . . ."

9. *The Horror Moves*

"WE MUST OVERTAKE it before it reaches the crossroads," shouted Little.

They were speeding by the sea, tearing at seventy miles an hour down a long, white road that twisted and turned between ramparts of sand. On both sides there towered dunes, enormous, majestic, morning stars a-gliter on the dark waters intermittently visible beyond their seaward walls. The horseshoe-shaped isthmus extended to six miles into the sea and then doubled back toward the Jersey coast. At the point where it changed its direction stood a crossroad, explicitly sign-posted with two pointing hands. One of these junctions led directly toward the mainland, the other into a dense, ocean-defiled waste, marshy and impregnable, a kind of morass where anything or any one might hide indefinitely.

And toward this retreat Chaugnar fled. For hours Little's car had pursued it along the tarred and macadamized roads that fringe the Jersey coast—over bridges and viaducts and across wastes of sand, in a straight line from Asbury Park to Atlantic City and then across country and back again to the coast, and now adown a thin terrain lashed by

Atlantic spray, deserted save for a few ramshackle huts of fishermen and a vast congregation of gulls.

Chaugnar Faugn had moved with unbelievable rapidity, from the instant when they had first encountered it crouching somnolently in the shadows beneath a deserted bathhouse at Long Branch and had turned the light on it and watched it awake to the moment when it had gone shambling away through the darkness its every movement had been ominous with menace.

Twice it had stopped in the road and waited for them to approach and once its great arm had raised itself against them in a gesture of malignant defiance. And on that occasion only the entropy machine had saved them. Its light Chaugnar could not bear, and when Little had turned the ray upon the creature's flanks the great obscene body had heaved and shuddered and a ghastly screeching had issued from its bulbous lips. And then forward again it had forged, its thick, stumpy legs moving with the rapidity of pistons—carrying it over the ground so rapidly that the car could not keep pace.

But always its tracks had remained visible, for a phosphorescence streamed from them, illuming its retreat. And always its hoarse bellowing could be heard in the distance, freighted with fury and a hatred incalculable. And by the stench, too, they trailed it, for all the air through which it passed was acridly defiled—pungent with an uncleanliness that evades description.

"It is infinitely old," cried Little as he manœuvred the car about the base of a sea-lashed dune. "As old as the earth's crust. Otherwise it would have crumbled. You saw how the bathhouse crumbled—how the shells beneath its feet dissolved and vanished. It is only its age that saves it."

"You had the light on it for five minutes," shouted Algernon. His voice was hoarse with excitement. "And it still lives. What can we do?"

"We must corner it—keep the light directed at it for—many minutes. To send it back we must decrease the random element in it by a billion years. It has remained substantially as it is now for at least that long. Perhaps longer."

"How many years of earth-time does the machine lop off a minute?" shouted Imbert.

"Can't tell exactly. It works differently with different objects. Metals, stone, wood all have a different entropy-rhythm. But roughly, it should reverse entropy throughout a billion years of earth-time in ten or fifteen minutes."

"There it is! " shouted Algernon. "It's reached the cross-roads. Look! "

Against a windshield glazed with seamist Imbert laid his forehead, peering with bulging eyes at the form of Chaugnar, phosphorescently illumed a quarter-mile before them on the road, and even as he stared the distance between the car and the loathsome horror diminished by fifty yards.

"It isn't moving," cried Little. He had half risen from his seat and was gripping the wheel as thought it were a living thing. "It's waiting for us. Turn on the light, sir. Quick! For God's sake! We're almost on top of it! "

Algernon fell upon his knees in the dark and groped about for the switch. The engine's roar increased as Little stepped furiously upon the accelerator. "The light, quick! " Little almost screamed the words.

Algernon's fingers found the switch and thrust it sharply

upward. There ensued the drone of revolving spheres. "It's moving again. God, it's moving! "

Algernon rose shakingly to his feet. "Where is it?" he shouted. "I don't see it! "

"It's making for the marshes," shouted Little. "Look.. Straight ahead, through here." He pointed toward a clear spot in the windshield. Craning hysterically, Algernon descried a phosphorescent bulk making off over the narrowest of the bisecting roads.

With a frantic spin of the wheel Little turned the car about and sent the speedometer soaring. The road grew narrower and more uneven as they advanced along it and the car careened perilously. "Careful," Algernon called out warningly. "We'll get ditched. Better slow up."

"No," cautioned Little, his voice sharp with alarm. "We can't stop now."

The light from the machine was streaming unimpeded into the darkness before them.

"Keep it trained on the road," shouted Little. "It would destroy a man in an instant."

They could smell the mud flats now. A pungent salty odour of stagnant brine and putrescent shellfish drifted toward them, whipped by the wind. A sickly yellow light was spreading sluggishly in the eastern sky. Across the road ahead of them a turtle shambled and vanished hideously in a flash.

"See that?" cried Little. "That's how Chaugnar would go if it wasn't as old as the earth."

"Be ready with the brakes," Algernon shouted back.

The end of the road had swept into view. It ran swiftly downhill for fifty yards and terminated in a sandy waste that was half submerged at its lower levels. The illumed bulk of Chaugnar paused for an instant on a sandy hillock. Then it moved rapidly downward toward the flats, arms spread wide, body swaying strangely, as though it were in awe of the sea.

Little steered the car to the side of the road and threw on the brakes. "Out—both of you!" he shouted.

Algernon descended to the ground and stood for an instant shakingly clinging to the door of the car. Then, in a sudden access of determination, he sprang back and began tugging at the machine, whilst Imbert strove valiantly to assist him.

There came a bellow from the great form that was advancing into the marsh. Algernon drew close to Little, and gripped him firmly by the arm. "Hadn't we better wait here?" he asked, his voice tight with strain. "It seems to fear the sea. We can entrench ourselves here and attack it with the light when it climbs back."

"No," Little's reply was emphatic. "We haven't a second to waste. It may—mire itself. It's too massive to flounder through the mud without becoming hopelessly bogged down. We'll drive it forward into the marsh."

Resolutely he stopped and beckoned to his companions to assist him in raising and supporting the machine. Dawn was spreading in the east, as the three men staggered downward over the sandy waste, a planet's salvation in the glittering shape they carried.

Straight into the morass they went, quaking with terror but impelled by a determination that was oblivious to caution. From Chaugnar there now came an insistent screeching and bellowing, a noise that smote so ominously on Algernon's ear that he wanted, desperately, to drop the machine and head back toward the car. But above the obscene bellowings of the horror rose Little's voice in courageous exhortation. "Don't stop for an instant," he cried. "We must keep it from circling back to the road. It will turn in a moment. It's sinking deeper and deeper. It will have to turn."

Their shoes sank into the sea-soaked marsh weeds, while luridly across the glistening morass streamed the greenish light from the machine, effacing everything in its path save the mud itself, which bubbled and heaved, made younger in an instant by ten thousand years. And then, suddenly, the great thing turned and faced them.

Knee-deep in the soft mud it turned, its glowing flanks quivering with ire, its huge trunk malignly upraised, a flail of flame. For an instant it loomed thus terribly menacing, the soul of all malignancy and horror, a cancerous cyclops oozing fetor. Then the light swept over it, and it recoiled with a convulsive trembling of its entire bulk. Though half mired, it retreated swayingly, and its bellows turned hoarse gurglings, such as no animal throat had uttered in all earth's eons of sentient evolution.

And then, slowly, it began to change. As the light streamed over and enveloped it, it began unmistakably to shrivel and darken.

"Keep the light steady," Little cried out, his voice tremulous with concern, his features set in an expression of utter revulsion.

Algernon and Imbert continued to advance with the machine, as sickened as Little was by what they saw but supported now by the disappearance of all uncertainty as to the truth of Little's claims.

And now that which had taken to itself an earth-form in eons primordial began awfully to disincarn and before

104

their gaze was enacted a drama so revolting as to imperil reason. A burning horror withdrew from its garments of clay and retraced in patterns of unspeakable dimness the history of its enshrinement. Not instantly had it incarned itself, but by stages slow and fantasmal and sickening. To ascend, Chaugnar had had to feast, not on men at first, for there were no men when it lay venomously outspread on the earth's crust, but on entities no less malignant than itself, the spawn of star-births incalculable. For before the earth cooled she had drawn from the skies a noxious progeny. Drawn earthward by her holocaust they had come, and relentlessly Chaugnar had devoured them.

And now as that which had occurred in the beginning was enacted anew these blasphemies were disgorged, and above the dark wrack defilement spread. And at last from a beast-shape to a jelly Chaugnar passed, a jelly enveloped in darting filaments of corpse-pale flame. For an instant it moved above the black marsh, as it had moved in the beginning when it had come from beyond the universe of stars to wax bestial in the presence of Man. And then the flames vanished and nothing remained but a cold wind blowing across the estuary from the open sea.

Little let out a great cry and Algernon released his hold on the machine and dropped to his knees on the wet earth Imbert, too, relinquished the machine but before doing so he shot back the lever at its base.

Only for an instant did the victory go unchallenged. For before the spheres on the machine had ceased to revolve, before even the light had vanished from the gleaming waste, the malignancy that had been Chaugnar Faugn reshaped itself in the sky above them.

Indescribably it loomed through the grey sea-mists, its

105

bulk magnified a thousandfold, its long, dangling trunk swaying slowly back and forth.

For an instant it towered above them, glaring venomously. Then, like a racer, it stooped and floundered forward and went groping about with its monstrous hands for the little shapes it hated. It was still groping when it dimmed and vanished into the depth of the hazy, dawn-brightened sky.

10. Little's Explanation

IT WAS THE FIFTH DAY since Chaugnar Faugn had been sent back through time. Algernon and Little sat in the latter's laboratory and discussed the destruction of the horror over cups of black coffee.

"You think, then, that the last manifestation we saw was a kind of spectral emanation, without physical substance."

"Not wholly, perhaps," replied Little. "An odour of putrefaction came from it. I should regard the phenomenon as a kind of tenuous reassembling rather than an apparition in a strict sense. Chaugnar had been incarnate for so long in the hideous shape with which we are familiar that its disembodied intelligence could reclothe itself in a kind of porous mimesis before it returned to its hyperdimensional sphere. So rapidly did our machine reverse entropy that perhaps tiny fragments of its terrestrial body survived, and these, by a tremendous exercise of will, it may have reassembled and, figuratively, *blown up*. That is to say, it may have taken these tiny fragments and so increased their porosity beyond the normal porosity of matter that they produced the cyclopean apparition we saw. All matter, you know, is tremendously porous, and if I could remove all the 'vacuums' from your body you would shrink to the size of a pin-head."

Algernon nodded, and was silent for a moment. Then he stood up, laid his coffee cup on the windowsill and crossed to where Little was sitting. "We agreed," he said, "that we wouldn't discuss Chaugnar further until . . . well, until we were in a little calmer frame of mind than we were a few days ago. It was a wise decision, I think. But I'm now so certain that what we both witnessed was not an illusion that I must insist you return an *honest* answer to two questions. I shall not expect a comprehensive and wholly satisfying explanation, for I'm aware that you are not completely sure yourself as to the exact nature of Chaugnar. But you have at least formed an hypothesis, and there are a good many things you haven't told me which I've earned the right to know."

"What do you wish to know?" Little's voice was constrained, reluctant.

"What destroyed the horror in the Pyrenees? Why were there no more massacres after—after that night?"

Little smiled wanly. "Have you forgotten the pools of black slime which were found on the melting snow a thousand feet above the village three days after we sent Chaugnar back?"

"You mean . . ."

Little nodded. "Chaugnar's kin, undoubtedly. They accompanied Chaugnar back, but left like their master, a few remainders. Little round pools of putrescent slime—a superfluity of rottenness that somehow resisted the entropy-reversing action of the machine."

"You mean that the machine sent entropy-reversing emanations half across the world?"

Little shook his head. "I mean simply that Chaugnar Faugn and its hideous brethren were *joined together* hyperdimensionally and that we destroyed them simultaneously. It is an axiom of virtually every speculative philosophy based on the newer physics and the concepts of non-Euclidean mathematics that we can't perceive the real *relations* of objects in the external world, that since our senses permit us to view them merely three-dimensionally we can't perceive the hyperdimensional links which unite them.

"If we could see the same objects—men, trees, chairs, houses—on a fourth-dimensional plane, for instance, we'd notice connections that are now wholly unsuspected by us. Your chair, to pick an example at random, may actually be joined to the window-ledge behind you or . . . to the Woolworth Building. Or you and I may be but infinitesimally tiny fragments of some gigantic monster occupying vast segments of space-time. You may be a mere excrescence on the monster's back, and I a hair of its head—I speak metaphorically, of course, since in higher dimensions of space-time there can be nothing but analogies to objects on the terrestrial globe—or you and I and all men, and everything in the world, every particle of matter, may be but a single fragment of this larger entity. If anything should happen to the entity you and I would *both* suffer, but as the monster would be invisible to us, no one —no one equipped with normal human organs of awareness—would suspect that we were suffering because we were parts of *it*. To a three-dimensional observer we should appear to be suffering from different causes and our invisible hyperdimensional *solidarity* would remain wholly unsuspected.

"If two people were thus hyperdimensionally joined, like Siamese twins, and one of them were destroyed by a machine similar to the one we used against Chaugnar Faugn, the other would suffer effacement at the same instant, though he were on the opposite side of the world."

Algernon looked puzzled.

"But why should the link be invisible? Assuming that Chaugnar Faugn and the Pyrenean horrors were hyper-dimensionally joined together—either because they were parts of one great monster, or merely because they were *one* in the hyperdimensional sphere, why should this hyper-dimensional connecting link be invisible to us?"

"Well—perhaps an analogy will make it clearer. If you were a *two* instead of a three-dimensional entity, and if, when you regarded objects about you—chairs, houses, animals—you saw only their length and breadth, you wouldn't be able to form any intelligible conception of their relations to other objects in the dimension you couldn't apprehend—the dimension of *thickness*. Only a portion of an ordinary three-dimensional object would be visible to you and you could only make a mystical guess as to how it would look with another dimension added to it. In that, to you, unperceivable dimension of thickness it might join itself to a thousand other objects and you'd never suspect that such a connection existed. You might perceive hundreds of flat surfaces about you, all discon-nected, and you would never imagine that they formed one object in the third dimension.

"You would live in a two-dimension world and when three-dimensional objects intruded into that world you

would be unaware of their true objective conformation—
or relatively unaware, for your perceptions would be perfectly valid so long as you remained two-dimensional.

"Our perceptions of three-dimensional world are only valid for that world—to a fourth-dimensional or fifth- or sixth-dimensional entity our conceptions of objects external to us would seem utterly ludicrous. And we know that such entities exist. Chaugnar Faugn was such an entity. And because of its hyperdimensional nature it was joined to the horror on the hills in a way we weren't able to perceive. We can perceive connections when they have length, breadth and thickness, but when a new dimension is added they pass out of our ken, precisely as a solid object passes out of the ken of an observer in a dimension lower than ours. Have I clarified your perplexities?"

Algernon nodded. "I think—yes, I am sure that you have. But I should like to ask you another question. Do you believe that Chaugnar Faugn is a transcendent world-soul endowed with a supernatural incorporeality, or just—just a material entity? I mean, was Ulman's priest right and was Chaugnar an incarnation of the Oneness of the Grahmic mysteries, the portentous all-in-all of theosophists and occulists, or merely a product of physical evolution on a plane incomprehensible to us?"

Little took a long sip of coffee and very deliberately lowered his head, as though he were marshalling his convictions for a debate. "I believe I once told you," he said at last, "that I didn't believe Chaugnar Faugn could be destroyed by any agent less transcendental than that which we used against it. It certainly wasn't protoplasmic or mineral, and no mechanical device not based on relativist concepts could have effected the dissolution we witnessed.

An infra-red ray machine, for instance, or a cyclotron would have been powerless to send it back. Yet despite the transcendental nature of even its carnate shell, despite the fact that even in its earth-shape it was fashioned of a substance unknown on the earth and that we can form no conception of its shape in the multidimensional sphere it now inhabits, it is my opinion that it is inherently, like ourselves, a circumscribed entity—the spawn of remote worlds and unholy dimensions, but a creature and not a creator, a creature obeying inexorable laws and occupying a definite niche in the cosmos.

"In a way we can never understand it had acquired the ability to roam and could incarn itself in dimensions lower than its own. But I do not believe it possessed the attributes of deity. It was neither beneficent nor evil, but simply amorally virulent—a vampire-like life form from beyond the universe of stars strayed by chance into our little, walled-in three-dimensional world. One unguarded gate may be standing ajar . . ."

"But do you believe that it actually made a race of men to serve it—that the Miri Nigri were fashioned from the flesh of primitive amphibians?"

Little frowned. "I don't know. Conditions on the cooling earth two billion years ago may once have been such that creations of that nature antedated the process of biological evolution with which we are familiar. And we may be sure that Chaugnar Faugn with its inscrutable endowments could have fashioned men-shapes had it so desired —could have fashioned them even from the planktonlike swarms of small organisms which must have drifted with the tides through the ancient oceans.

Little lowered his voice and looked steadily at Algernon.

"Some day," he murmured, "Chaugnar may return. We sent it back through time, but in five thousand or a hundred thousand years it may return to ravage. Its return will be presaged in dreams, for when its brethren stirred restlessly on the Spanish hills both I and Hsieh Ho were disturbed in our sleep by harbingers from beyond. Telepathically Chaugnar spoke to sleeping minds, and if it returns it will speak again, for Man is not isolated among the sentient beings of earth but is linked to all that moves in hyper-dimensional continuity."

FLAME OF LIFE

FIFTY-THREE THOUSAND miles above the surface of earth, Thomas Marshall had felt almost godlike, but now he was a shy young man, taking a shower in an airport locker room. He stood in the buff, while the torrent descended on him, seeing again the sun glowing in the black heavens —a dull red disk with a visible corona, and all about it, white stars glowing.

He had come back alive, the first human being to be exposed to cosmic rays at that height, and he was a popular hero; even Radio Moscow expressed congratulations. But Marshall didn't feel heroic.

He was just the kind of man who could do this sort of thing, the solitary sort, the shy type, the lonely kind. They'd given him leave for a few days; they'd arranged for him to get to New York quietly, a police escort whisking him away from the crowd that surrounded the plane, and sneaking him into the airport lockers. He'd have to make some public appearances, he knew; but tonight, at least, he'd be by himself.

Which was worse, he wondered—the crowds, or the loneliness?

115

He stepped from the shower and towelled himself dry. He dressed quickly, pulled the hat down over his eyes, loosened the knot of his tie and lit a cigarette. He paced impatiently about the locker room, cursing softly under his breath.

A minute ticked away into a steam-vapourish eternity. Then the door opened and an airport official peered into the room.

"Your car is waiting, Mr. Marshall," he said. "It's a limousine with drawn blinds. A state trooper will accompany you."

Thomas Marshall groaned. "The blinds are okay," he said. "But I don't want a police escort."

He had his way. Five minutes later, he left the airport in a long, black car that purred, but with no motorcycles trailing him. Being a somebody had its advantages. His slightest whim was satisfied. The car picked up speed as it left the airport. It was soon an ebon cylinder flashing through the night.

A wide, macadamized state highway stretched between the airport and the city. It bisected a long stretch of level marshland, ascended in a gradient over meadows that shone with a blue lustre in the light of a spectral moon, tunnelled under viaducts that quivered with the passing of ponderous trucks, and entered the city through a region of docks and abysmal slums.

The change occurred gradually. It began when he left the airport, making his shift about restlessly in the depths of the car. He was shivering violently when the damp marsh air assailed his nostrils. When he passed between the blue-lit meadows, he stared excitedly out of the window. When the dismal dwellings of the waterfront

116

region loomed up on all sides of him, he seized the communication tube and shouted to the driver: "Stop here. Stop at once."

The driver swerved to the kerb and stepped on the brakes. There was a squealing of tyres as the car came to an abrupt halt beneath the red-brick façade of an enormous, deserted warehouse.

With incredible agility, Marshall leapt from the limousine. He stood for a moment teetering on the kerb, his eyes shining, his breath coming fast. The edifice that towered up behind him contrasted strangely with the streamlined magnificence of the limousine.

Broken and blankly staring windows gave the warehouse an air of desolation and squalor which was accentuated by the weather-eroded bricks of its precipitous façade. Utterly clifflike it seemed, a cyclopean stone barrier blotting out the stars.

Beneath it swarmed the furtive, ugly night life of the slums. The driver leaned out of the car and stared at Marshall on the kerb. His eyes widened; his mouth fell open. Utter terror shone for an instant in his gaze.

Marshall said: "I'll walk the rest of the way, Collier. You can drive the car back to the airport, if you wish."

The driver cried: "Good God, sir, the light . . ."

"The light? What light? Are you crazy, Collier?"

The driver nodded. "I must be, you seem to be all . . ."

"Never mind, Collier. Just leave me."

The driver said: "You bet I will." The car swerved out into the centre of the street and shot away into the night.

Marshall threw his arms up over his head. He waltzed about on his toes. He shouted; he laughed. A savage exaltation had him in thrall.

A reeling drunk emerged from a dark alley near at hand. He swayed toward Marshall, cursing. Then suddenly he stopped, stared. His eyes got too big for his face.

Thomas Marshall began to run. He ran swiftly along the narrow pavement, keeping close to the warehouse. He ran exultantly through the sordid slum. He encircled a lamppost and brushed swiftly past an old woman who stared. He tripped over an alley cat and went sprawling. The cat screeched, erected its tail and backed away, saliva drooling from its bared teeth.

Laughing, Marshall picked himself up. He brushed himself off and started talking to himself. "It's just nerves, I guess. The long strain, ten hours of strain. But it's incredible how light-headed I feel. I could hug and kiss that old woman and she's as ugly as sin."

The old woman was backed against the warehouse, her scrawny hands clutching at her throat. She was staring at him and shaking. All the blood had drained from her face. A shabby shawl dangled from her bony, emaciated shoulders. Her skirt was torn and mud-bedraggled. She was so old she seemed ageless—ageless and incredibly ugly—a fragile, desiccated shell.

Marshall murmured: "It's incredible. She didn't seem as old as that a moment ago. She didn't seem . . ."

Suddenly he felt the muscles tightening along his jaw.

The old woman was shrinking before his eyes. The flesh of her face was shrivelling, darkening. Her clutching, bony hands became destitute of flesh. Her eyes burned like tapers of flame in the depths of her skull-like face.

And then, suddenly, her face was a skull—a fleshless skull surmounting a skeleton body against the bloodhued bricks of the warehouse.

A cold chill itched across Marshall's scalp. He wiped a hand across his brow and staggered back into the gutter. The skeleton image did not pursue him. It began to dwindle and dissolve. It became a nebulous white blur in the wan light of the street lamps, a vaguely articulated shadow-shape that hovered for an instant upright in the gloom.

The next instant, it was gone. Between Marshall and the warehouse stretched merely the narrow pavement and the small, elusive shadows of the night.

He stood for a moment giddily swaying in the gutter, feeling a constriction about his throat, his tongue parching as he strove desperately to summon reason to his aid.

It was an illusion, of course, an illusion of sense. From vague shadows, he had conjured up a fantastic shape that resembled a shrivelled old woman. Seemingly, it had the same reality as the bricks of the warehouse and the cat which had tripped him. But a strong illusion . . .

Perhaps it was more than an illusion! —an actual hallucination, perhaps. He had read somewhere that hallucinations could occur in all the senses simultaneously. Such images were more real than reality. They had a terrible clarity; they burned themselves into the senses in filaments of flame.

What was he muttering to himself? He was behaving like an idiot!

He drew himself up. He stepped back onto the pavement, squared his shoulders. He was beginning to feel light-headed again. His terror was dwindling. He felt a giddiness sweeping over him, a reckless defiance which banished fear.

He began to walk. Presently, he was running again. He was nearly at the end of the block when a flash of sudden light leapt out at him, half-blinding him. He whirled about in sudden dismay. Confronting him was a shimmering oblong of glass that blazed with little, weaving coruscations of light.

The window was unbroken. It was low down, on a level with his chest and not more than eight feet from the northern extremity of the warehouse. It was one of the few unbroken windows in the great, clifflike building

For an instant, he stood rigid and appalled, staring— staring! Mirrored in the tall window was the image of a man, the image of himself. Spirals of white and saffron flame streamed from his head and shoulders, aureoling him in a blinding incandescence!

He was literally blanketed in flames that danced and swirled continuously about the upper portion of his body! He could not see his limbs in the glass. Tremulously, he raised his hands and looked at them. They were faintly luminous, but not ablaze.

Utter consternation engulfed him. In blind terror, he turned from the window and tottered along the street Twice he stumbled and nearly fell.

He was afire! —yet he felt no pain, no searing torment as he reeled drunkenly through the night.

How he reached the wharf, he never knew. There were intervals of terror and confusion when he was obscurely aware of his surroundings alternated with a blackness that blotted out the world. He seemed at times to be running, at times to be staggering in circles through the shadow- thronged murk. He had a vague recollection of cries of fright, of scurrying human shapes.

His faculties were confused for a long while. It was not until he found himself on the wharf that his mind became lucid again and reality assumed sharp and agonizing contours.

He found himself standing on the wharf gazing down at a gleaming, black expanse that mirrored all the stars of heaven. He could hear the murmur of the tides as they swirled and eddied about rotting pier-heads and sucked at barnacle-encrusted piles. An odour of brine assailed his nostrils. Far out over the water, a tug boat shrilled.

Slowly, he raised his hands and stared at them. They were still faintly luminous, nebulously aglow. He leaned out over the wharf and gazed down into the dark water. In the depths of the water, he saw human shoulders that blazed, a human head aureoled in flame! Despair enveloped him like a shroud.

The girl was standing a few feet away on the opposite side of the wharf. Her head was lowered in sombre contemplation of the dark water. Her back was turned to him; she seemed unaware of his presence.

Her face was deathly pale in the moonlight. It was a very lovely face. The girl was of medium height, with fair, exquisite features. The moonlight haloed her red-gold hair, dappled her white throat, descended in silver curlicues over her slender body.

She was staring intently at the black water, her body swaying a little. Suddenly she moved to the edge of the wharf, cried out in despair and raised her arms. The next instant she was gone.

Marshall stared thunder-struck. The water below whirled dizzily to his gaze. The star reflections were shattered as though some cosmic hammer had shattered the mirror of the sea.

Sweat started out over Marshall's face. His horror forgotten, he bent swiftly. With feverish fingers, he unlaced and removed his shoes, ripped off his coat. As he dived from the wharf, the girl's thrashing body seemed to spin through an ebon vortex immediately beneath him.

Straight into the vortex he plunged, his body bent like a bow. He went down into cold blackness. His body sliced through the water in a perfect arc and emerged twenty feet from the wharf. Frantically, he trod water, turning swiftly about and searching the gleaming expanse for the girl's struggling form.

Presently he saw her. She was bobbing about under the wharf, her face obscurely visible in a swirl of foam. Swiftly, he swam toward her. Their bodies collided in a churning maelstrom. He turned on his back, grasped her about the waist, and drew her relentlessly to his side.

She struggled a little as he swam backward with powerful leg strokes. In a moment, he had reached the sloping stone underpinnings of the wharf. He pulled himself to safety with his free arm, dragging the girl up beside him. He stared at her apprehensively as she sagged on a horizontal ledge of stone, her back resting against a huge, circular pier head. Her hair was a sodden mass, her face utterly bloodless. She was choking and gasping for breath.

Presently, her breathing shortened into sighs. She shifted about on the slippery stone ledge, raised her eyes and stared at him. Her white face seemed to go a shade whiter. She raised her hands to her throat in terror.

Marshall said: "Do not be afraid. The radiance is just —just fluorescence. I am a chemical worker in a laboratory. Radiant particles lodged in my skin. It will wear off in a little while."

He lied feverishly, hoping, praying that she would believe

122

him. He needed someone to cling to in his despair—some-one warm and human and alive.

The terror went out of her eyes. She slumped on the ledge, her shoulders drooping, her lips twisting.

"Forgive me," she said. "The radiance frightened me. For a moment I thought . . ."

Marshall laughed hoarsely. "You thought me Lucifer in shining raiment, perhaps?"

A wan smile crossed the girl's face. "Why not an angel of light? You risked your life to save me. Only I—I wanted to die."

He was studying the girl closely now. Her clothes were pathetically shabby. She was wearing cotton socks and shoes with plugged soles.

Compassion shone in his gaze. "Poverty?"

The girl nodded. "It nearly always is, isn't it?"

"Yes," he said. "Nearly always. You look half starved. How long since you've had a decent meal?"

The girl said: "Three days."

"And how long since you've had a job?"

She smiled again. "Four months. I guess I'm not very brave."

"Nonsense," he said. "I can tell by your eyes that you're brave—and much too young to die."

She said again: "I wanted to die."

"I know, but you'll feel better when you've had something to eat."

She was looking at him queerly now. Suddenly she said: "You're Thomas Marshall, aren't you?"

Momentarily he had forgotten that he was Thomas Marshall. The girl's loveliness had absorbed him to the exclusion of all else.

123

Her recognition dismayed him. He said, falteringly. "Yes, I'm Marshall—but I know what it means to be wretched and lonely and—lost."

The girl stared at him incredulously. "Why should you be lonely? You have everything. Wealth, fame . . ."

He smiled bitterly. "I'll tell you about that when you're warm again. We'll find a restaurant and talk. You're shivering."

They found an all-night cafeteria located on a dingy, winding waterfront street. It was a welcome haven after their strenuous ascent in the cold darkness to the wharf. Compared to the wind that pursued them as they fled to cover, it seemed very warm and friendly.

The proprietor was a little gnomelike man with an atrophied sense of curiosity. He raised his eyes and nodded when they entered, passing them a menu over a long counter. He scarcely seemed to notice their drenched and dripping clothes.

The girl sat on a revolving stool facing her companion, her face still deathly pale, her eyes shining.

"The fluorescence doesn't show in the light," she said.

His hand went out and gripped her wrist. "I'll get you a job," he said. "Tomorrow. A real job. You won't—ever go out on that wharf again. Promise me you won't."

"I promise," she said.

"You might tell me your name."

"Barbara Ellison," she said. "I am twenty-three. I spent four years in a business college before I came East. I was born in the Middle West, but I came East to look for a job in an office. I didn't get one."

"You'll have one tomorrow," he said. "Now let's eat."

Standing on the counter before them were two cups of

coffee and a platter of doughnuts. The girl took one of the doughnuts and broke it apart with fingers that trembled a little. She said: "I'm grateful, believe me."

"Nonsense," he said, feeling a little of the horror stealing over him again, feeling that she must never leave him. "I'm grateful to you. You'll never know how grateful."

"But why? What did I do?"

"You risked your life—your life that belongs to so many people, and all for a girl with no courage at all."

He said: "It takes courage to have too much to live for."

Her face was very close now and her breath fanned his cheek.

In confusion, he picked up a doughnut and raised a steaming cup of coffee to his lips. "I'll take mine black," he said, and smiled at her when she pushed a pitcher of cream toward him.

Then, suddenly, the smile vanished from his lips. The girl beside him was changing before his eyes! She was changing, receding into a nebulous haze. She seemed to be shrinking too—growing smaller, her limbs shortening, her face becoming plump and rosy!

Horror blazed over him again. He turned as white as a sheet and began to tremble. The girl seemed to be still sipping her coffee, but her body was enveloped in a nebulous mist that swirled up about her in rippling waves. Her clothes were concealed by the white opacity. Obscurely through the mist he saw short, plump legs that dangled and above them the rosy, innocent face of a little child!

She was a child of four, a cherubic infant sipping a cup of coffee almost as large as its face!

Then, slowly, the mist evaporated and the girl was beside

125

him again. She was staring at him with troubled eyes. She said: "Why did you start so? You frightened me."

Sweat beaded Marshall's forehead. He passed a hand across his damp brow, stared at the huge silver coffee percolator which stood at the end of the counter and the proprietor dozing in shadows a few feet away. The proprietor was leaning over an oyster bar at the rear of the restaurant, his eyes three-fourths shut, his elbows supporting him as he drowsed.

He had not changed at all—neither had the coffee percolator, the long counter, the dingy plate glass windows and all the rest of the shabby little restaurant. Only the girl had changed—for a brief, appalling instant.

White-lipped and trembling, Marshall picked up the cheques.

"Shall we go now, Barb—Barbara?" he said.

The girl glanced swiftly up at him. A strange tenderness came into her face. She said, simply: "Yes, if you wish."

He was trembling uncontrollably when they left the restaurant. As soon as they emerged into the street, she linked her arm in his and stared up into his white, tormented face, her eyes luminous with concern.

"Are you ill, Thomas?" she asked.

He shook his head, and walked with her in silence through the chill greyness that precedes dawn. Their linked shadows danced grotesquely on dim-lit pavements and flickered over deserted, tenement-house doorways.

Suddenly he said: "Where do you live, Barbara?"

She mentioned a mean street on the north side of the city. Marshall was familiar with the north side. Relief surged up in him as he visualized long rows of shabby-genteel rooming houses. The neighbourhood was desolate

126

and down at heel—a dismal region of decaying brown stones dating back to the Mauve Decade. But it was not a slum.

It was about a fifteen minutes' walk to the girl's home. Marshall seized her hand and held it tightly while they threaded their way out of the waterfront maze into a region where the squalor was less oppressive.

He did not speak again until they arrived at the high stoop of the rooming house. The flames which poured from him enveloped the girl without harming her, swirling up about her slender body in a golden blaze. She was clinging to him and shivering, her face illumined by the lambent glare.

His fingers tightened on her hand. He said: "I'll phone you in the morning, Barbara. Promise me you'll go straight to bed."

She said: "I promise. Thomas." But she did not move away from him. Instead, she moved closer to him.

She moved tremulously closer until she was in his arms. He cried out in sudden wonder and strained her to him, all else forgotten. The horror of the enveloping glow, the strange confusion which had descended upon his faculties —all was forgotten, swallowed up in a blinding ecstasy such as he had never known.

She was in his arms and he was kissing her hair and lips and eyes. The bleak rooming house towered up behind them—unseen. He was only aware of her warm and clinging arms and the wild beating of his heart.

When he released her, her eyes were glowing. She turned and ran swiftly up the stoop into a dim-lit vestibule. Stunned, tremulous, he watched her fumbling in her bag for a key. Suddenly she turned and blew him a kiss.

"Tomorrow," she called, and was gone.

He stood for an instant staring up at the shabby façade above him, scarcely seeing it, thinking only of the girl who had vanished.

Suddenly he felt a chill creeping over him. The dismal brownstone was becoming nebulous, was receding into mist.

It was unmistakably dwindling, receding! All about it whirled a tenuous haze. Gradually, a new mass seemed to collect behind it—a smaller, more graceful mass that emerged obscurely from whiteness.

Marshall was held transfixed. The impossible was happening before his eyes! A huge, substantial house was dissolving and another taking its place. As he watched, the new dwelling assumed sharp and distinctive contours.

Before him on the deserted street stood a three-storey house of Georgian brick with antique chimney pots and glowing, square-paned windows. Silhouetted in its fan-lighted doorway was the figure of a young man with pale, aristocratic features.

The young man was startlingly attired in sky-blue small-clothes and snow-white periwig. Silver buckles gleamed on his satin pumps and he wore silken breeches. As Marshall stared, there appeared beside him in the doorway a slender, white-haired girl dressed in the costume of the eighteenth century.

Marshall cried out in stunned wonder! The mist was returning again, was obscuring the outlines of the second dwelling. Gradually it receded until it was a vague, amorphous blur.

In the depths of the blur, an enormous shape was stirring. As the second dwelling dwindled, a Gargantuan animal

128

form loomed obscurely out of the mist. Gigantically, it towered in the still night, while on both side of it the air seemed to quiver and recede with a curious glimmering over silent houses of decaying brownstone.

In the mist-filled void between the houses loomed the terrifying apparition of an enormous cat. It was like no cat Marshall had ever seen before. It was fifteen feet in height and it sat immobile on its haunches menacingly regarding him!

It was snarling, hissing at him, its eyes glowing balefully in the darkness—but it was not so much the appalling size of the animal or its menacing ferocity that filled Marshall with blind, unreasoning terror.

What sent him reeling back across the gutter, his mind a jumbled ferment of incredulity and horror, was the cat's long curving tusks! Curving out from the creature's feral jaws were two enormous slivers of ivory that glowed dully in the darkness.

Mercifully, the mist returned, obscuring the monstrous feline—but Marshall did not wait for the shape to vanish. He turned and reeled blindly along the street.

He was still reeling when he woke David Rand at three in the morning. He appeared at Rand's door dishevelled, wild-eyed, his face the colour of tallow.

David Rand was Marshall's only friend in the city.

Calm and scientific was David Rand, eyes palely discerning behind steel-rimmed spectacles, hair close-cropped, long, sallow face impeccable in its poise and restraint.

He was Marshall's counsellor in boyhood, the confidant of his years of struggle—ten years older than Marshall, but still on the pleasant side of forty—biochemist, physicist, astronomer—dabbler in a dozen sciences, but a competent and gifted dabbler.

He met Marshall in pyjamas, his face showing surprise and concern, guided him in to a spacious, book-lined study and mixed him a whiskey and soda.

Five minutes later, Marshall was talking. He sat in an old-fashioned easy chair, leaning forward a little, his eyes glowing feverishly. He stopped occasionally to puff on a cigarette. Occasionally, he sipped at the glass in his hand.

Rand listened in silence to Marshall's incredible recital, nodding his head thoughtfully from time to time. Finally, Marshall ceased to talk. He sank back exhausted and stared at his listener in mute despair.

Rand sat regarding him for an instant in silence, his fingers plucking at the grey frogs on his black silk pyjamas. When he spoke, his pale eyes were glowing.

"There is much, of course, that we still do not understand about the strange new reality which we are accustomed to refer to as space-time.

"But this thought has occurred to me, Thomas. You ascended fifty-three thousand miles; cosmic rays and the rays of infra-light—are potent in the upper ionosphere."

He stroked his chin thoughtfully. "You are of course familiar with the speculations of that gifted biochemist, Dr. Crille. Crille believes that all our body cells are endowed with microscopic suns, radiogens, continually radiating microspecks of searing light.

"He believes that life itself is a byproduct of billions of tiny suns which suck energy from light—of tiny suns that glow in us, microscopic batteries of life."

He paused an instant, then resumed: "Now consider the mysterious new space-time of the physicist—of Einstein,

Eddington, De Sitter and the rest. Our awareness of space-time is limited because human perception is three dimensional. We do not perceive time as an aspect of space. But we know that time is an aspect of space! If human perception were four dimensional, we would not be aware of time as a flowing of events.

"We would not be aware of time at all. The past, the present, and perhaps the future would exist as static realities. We could examine one segment of space-time and see the past, another segment and see the present. I am not so sure about the future.

"But space-time would exist as a definite entity—timeless, static. All the past would exist in that entity—all the past, the present, and perhaps all the future.

"To express it differently, we would perceive space as it really is—and that includes time. Space-time is simply true of four-dimensional space. Time is simply an aspect of true space.

"We cannot perceive true space because our faculties are biologically limited. But suppose we intensified our life forces. Suppose we transcended our protoplasmic limitations!

"Assume that life is a byproduct of the tiny suns in us, the radiogens. Suppose those radiogens sucked new energy from the cosmic rays, expanded, became Novas in our body cells. You understand—new suns, brighter suns."

Marshall was leaning forward in his chair now, his face strangely taut. "You mean," he said, "that up in the ionosphere . . ."

Rand nodded. "The cosmic rays charged your radiogens, which are microscopic batteries of life, with undreamed-of new energies! They flared more brightly in you, Thomas.

131

That would explain the glow, the fierce exaltation that swept over you, the desire to run and shout.

"Life burned more fiercely in you, Thomas. Your faculties expanded. You transcended your biological limitations. You perceived the fourth-dimension or true space—only momentarily, of course—in flickers, but you perceived the past, which still exists in true space. You had momentary, evanescent glimpses of the past.

"You saw the girl you spoke of as a little child. And you—wait a minute, Thomas. You did see the future! The future must exist. You saw the old woman shrivel and becomes a fleshless skeleton!"

Rand sprang up and strode about the room. "You saw the future! Do you realize what that means, Thomas, the implications?"

Marshall did not reply. When Rand saw how pale Marshall had become he sat down abruptly.

"It was chiefly the past you saw," he said, "sporadically, in flashes. You saw an eighteenth century house. Then you went back across wide wastes of years. You saw—a sabre-tooth tiger, a Machaerodus!—the largest, most sinister cat that ever walked the earth. You went back to the dim Eocene, to the age of the asphalt pits!"

Marshall felt very weak, tired, soul-sick and appalled.

He said: "But when Barbara became a little child, the restaurant did not recede or change. And when the house vanished, the street and the adjoining houses remained unchanged. And when Barbara was really a child, she was somewhere else in the world—not sitting beside me on a stool. Yet I saw her sitting there."

Rand said: "You're assuming that relationships in space-

132

time or true space are similar to relationships in our three-dimensional space—but it is an unlikely assumption. With the expansion of your faculties of perception, all relationship would change.

"We can only speculate as to just how they would change. It is probably that human beings preserve a definite continuity in true space which transcends their orientation in our space. You saw the girl sitting beside you because her past in true space was not chained down to her actual position when she was really a child in our space.

"Remember that plants, animals, and human beings are complex examples of entropic inversion. Entropy, as you know, means dissolution, disintegration. The universe as a whole is running down—but organic life is not. Organic life is building up, swimming against the swift entropic currents. It is possible that living organisms maintain a certain integrity in true space that makes them independent of our space when you perceive them as space-time units."

Suddenly Rand stood up again. His eyes were glowing. "Thomas," he said. "You have no idea how I envy you. Never before, in the whole history of our race, has a man been so gloriously privileged. You are no longer a wretched Earth bound biped akin to the apes! You have become godlike in your perceptions! "

Marshall groaned. "I do not want to be godlike, Rand. I want to be a normal human being again, not enveloped in flames, with all the world unstable about me. Rand, what am I to do . . .?"

Rand's impassivity was completely gone now. He strode

up and down the room, no longer able to control himself. Suddenly he whirled on Marshall.

"It is regrettable that the flames you spoke of are invisible in this light. I must see them. Thomas, I am going to turn out the light."

Marshall leapt up in protest, but before he could reach Rand's side, the other had stepped to the wall and switched off all the illumination in the room.

Utter darkness engulfed the two men. Rand could hear Marshall's agitated breathing and Marshall was aware of Rand moving about close to the wall. But utter darkness engulfed them. There was no light at all in the room!

Suddenly the light was on again. Rand was staring at Marshall with set lips. He seemed shaken, disappointed. He said: "You are no longer enveloped in flames, Thomas."

Marshall swayed a little. "You mean, you think . . ."

Rand nodded. "You are obviously normal again. You have had your wish. You have ceased to be godlike. Evidently, the radiogens flared with fierce new energies and then burned themselves out—or rather, dwindled to normal tiny suns again."

He was scowling disappointedly, as one who regretted to admit an unwelcome and unpleasant truth.

"It is significant that you were not immediately luminous. Evidently, you were flooded with rays, drenched by your ten hours high above Earth. It is probable that the radiogens absorbed the energy slowly, flared into brief novæ, and then dwindled again to the smaller suns of normal protoplasm."

The colour crept back into Marshall's cheeks. He straightened, seemed to increase in height. He said:

134

"Nothing has changed in this room, nothing. The other changes occurred swiftly—at fifteen-minute intervals. For over an hour, there has been no change at all."

Rand nodded. "I am quite sure you are normal again," he said. "You are restored. It is a pity—a great and tragic pity! For a brief hour, you were godlike. You could even see into the future and predict human events. You might have altered the destiny of our race."

Marshall said: "I am godlike now! A man in love is very close to the eternal."

"In love," said Rand. "I had forgotten. In love, Thomas?"

But Marshall did not hear him. He saw again moonlight haloing red-gold hair, dappling a white throat. He saw her face again, luminous with tenderness. He saw her standing in a dim-lit vestibule, waving at him. He heard her whisper: "Tomorrow, Thomas. Tomorrow!"

Happiness enveloped him like a flame, swirling up about him in a golden blaze.

GIANT IN THE FOREST

CLARICE SAID, "Peter, I feel so sorry for that poor little Martian in Ward C. You don't know what it means to be a telepath, and have to brood over the pain and shock in other minds."

She shook down a thermometer and placed it in a sterile metal case, her eyes pleading. "Couldn't you take a slight risk, and certify him as healed? He wants so desperately to go to the stars again."

"He was in a bad accident," I said. "The broken bones have to knit—"

Her eyes grew accusing. "He's almost healed . . . I'm sure of it. Why do you have to be such a perfectionist?"

I looked at my darling, serene and beautiful in her blue nurse's uniform, and pictured her sitting in candlelight in a smoky old restaurant, her hand tight in mine while I whispered into her ear.

That aspect of her wasn't quite in harmony with the cold grey walls of the hospital room, but it warmed the inner man.

"Ulno Drook has a first-rate mind and he's bound to get all kinds of honours," I said. "When you get to feeling sorry for him, just remember that the Third Martian Treaty guarantees Martians full equality with us in all scientific pursuits."

I patted her shoulder. "That's all that matters—to feel a sense of unity in achievement, to know you're respected as an equal. Martian bones are more brittle than ours and take longer to mend. And Drook's a telepath, sure; he's wide open to pain and grief when he's in close proximity to humans. But nature's inequalities are trivial in themselves. Drook can take it like the brave little guy he is."

"Well—at least go downstairs and have another talk with him," my darling urged. "He worships you, Peter."

"Does he now!"

"He really does, Peter."

I smiled at her and gave her arm a squeeze. "Tonight at eight," I said. "See you then."

The warmth, the glow was momentary. I walked out into the corridor with a stethoscope draped around my neck, a man in the image of a living human being, but feeling more like a mummy from an ancient Peruvian salt mine. We worked around the clock at *Explorers' Aid*, but sometimes we run out of time and have to manufacture a little on the quiet.

I found Drook in Ward C, sitting before an easel with a slender paint-brush in his hand. To keep his mind off his troubles the recreational director had taught him to paint like Gauguin.

Gauguin, it seems, was a painter who'd made quite a splash on Earth four centuries ago. Strong and proud and confident, Gauguin had painted women in barbaric costumes on long, golden afternoons, his palette aflame with hot jungle colours.

Getting the bodies of the Earth women right had been a little difficult for Drook because they didn't inspire in him any frenzies of delight. He'd simply imagined Earth women as they must have looked to Gauguin and painted them unabashed.

"Splendid, Ulno Drook!" I said. "You're making real progress."

He swung about, his big grey ears flapping and his gnome-face breaking into a smile. "You like it, Peter?"

"I like *her*," I said. "How did you ever learn to paint like that?"

"Anything Gauguin could do, I can do better," Drook said. "He had a great natural gift for creation, but he did not know how to make a human woman attractive to more than this type of man or that type of man. You have to be a telepath to widen the appeal."

His big ears drooped and a spasm of pain crossed the gnome-features. "Someone is suffering in the next ward," he said. "An accident case. Peter, I'm well enough to leave."

He shivered and gripped my wrist with his skinny fingers, his eyes imploring. "Take me out of here, Peter!"

Before I could reply the communicator globe lighted up, and a voice said: "Calling Dr. Jarvan. Dr. Jarvan, come to Ward E. immediately please. That is all."

Drook released my wrist, and I could tell by his expression that he had conquered his fear, and had something important to tell me. But all he said was: "Your brother is back from the stars, Peter."

Not how badly Seaton had been hurt, or even whether I could count on finding him alive. Drook pretended not to know, and I had to get the details from the nurse by phone on my way upstairs.

It wasn't too bad. Seaton was still conscious and he had sent for me himself.

Seaton had come back alive from the stars.

The walk to the stars was tremendous. It was a brief walk, and your feet hardly moved at all. One minute you'd be with friends, warm and secure and very sure of yourself. Saying goodbye to a dark-eyed girl perhaps, or holding in your arms a rather pathetic little figure wishing you luck.

The next you'd be collapsing into nothingness, your body and mind and hopes of eternity transferred from one vibrating metal disk to another vibrating disk across tens of thousands of light years. One step forward into the teleport; for an instant brief as a dropped heartbeat you ceased to be a man with the blood warm in your veins, and became a swirl of antigravitics in the chill gulfs between the stars.

It was not always a safe walk; despite every safety device which human genius could devise, accidents happened. Sometimes the transmission field blanked out, a gap formed, and human blood and bone ran like quick-silver into light millennia beyond the reach of human colonization. Sometimes the scanning mechanism failed, and an explorer emerged from a teleport shattered in body and mind. And for a few, the walk was over before it began.

My brother Seaton was one of the lucky ones. A shouting dishevelled Goliath he was, six feet five in his stockings, and he'd come back wild-eyed and delirious and wiping blood from his mouth. On the strength of his injuries they'd put him to bed, and given him a pretty, red-haired nurse;

they'd swabbed a space for needles, and then, at his own request, they'd sent for me.

As I strode along I thought back to when the first explorer went out into space and the first physician had been born to look after him. I'd never fired a gun, and all of my adventures came to me secondhand. But every time the dawn came up I counted myself the luckiest lad alive.

I wondered if Seaton would calm down when he saw me. I shut my eyes and pictured him walking through an unexplored wilderness where the Milky Way dimmed to a thin sprinkling of stars. Strange, vermilion-crested birds flaunted their plumage from every thicket, and rippling flashes of sunlight played over his tousled head and broad, straight shoulders.

Surely to explore a new world was to be a god! I thought of the men who had gone first in ships, travelling at many times the speed of light and letting fall from the blurring rim of overdrive the teleports which now dotted the planets of a thousand suns.

I thought of them and pitied them. They had paved the way and their rewards had been great. But surely to go alone was to know a far greater intoxication. It was the old primeval human dream recaptured in an age of scientific fulfilment. One lone man against the stars, pitting his intelligence and naked strength against the mystery and terror of the universe.

Its beauty too. Its terrible beauty that could wean a man from tilled fields and orchard hillsides, and make him dream of vast jungles, star-girded, tumbling into night a thousand light years from Sol.

The hospital room smelled faintly of antiseptics. I entered and shut the door quietly, knowing full well that a man could come back from the stars feeling as strong as an ox, and be dead in twenty minutes from parathyroid shock.

The red-haired nurse, who might have been the twin of a girl Seaton had been carrying the torch for a month before, turned quickly when she heard my footsteps on the tiled floor. The room was lighted by a warm glow from the wall panels, and her hair flamed as she turned; for an instant I found myself envying Seaton, without quite understanding why.

Seaton was sitting up straight, and when he saw me he let out a great shout. "Peter, lad, come here and let me look at you!"

I went over to him, nodding at the nurse who was trying to look professional, and gave him a gentle poke in the ribs. I grinned, and did my best to make him think he'd be out of bed in an hour.

My brother Seaton. Thick black hair he had, almost as coarse as a wolf's pelt; his eyes were dark and piercing, and nothing you could say to him could tame him when he wanted to behave like a wildman.

You'd never think he was a gentle scholar who could reel off the weight of every known element, determine a spectrum line to within one five-millionth of an inch, and outsmart me in a game of chess.

"You came through raving," I said.

He laughed. "I'm as fit as a fiddle now, Peter. It was just the scanners. They jolted me up like a thousand wild horses shooting sparks from their manes."

"I'm checking you over anyway," I said. "Open your shirt."

I was pressing the stethoscope to his chest when he said

142

in a low, earnest whisper: "Peter, lad, how would you like to go where you'd be free to help people in a really big way?"

He told me then about the world he'd just left. Callix Six was an Earthlike planet inhabited by a fair-skinned race of humans who did not differ from us in any way. A stricken race, desperately in need of medical aid. A great and consuming weariness had come upon them, and they went about their tasks with a groping uncertainty, and sank down exhausted in the doorways of their homes long before the setting of the sun.

"Peter, I want to tell you about them. You know there have been periods in human history when everything ugly seems to vanish like a bad dream. Take the Homeric world, for instance. We think of it as half-mythical, bathed in a light that never was on sea or land. Actually there must have been a period in the development of ancient Greece when conditions were very much as Homer described them.

"The great golden city-states already existed in embryo, so to speak, and the Greeks had been freed from the harshness and cruelty of barbarism. But they had not yet taken on the crushing burdens of civilization.

"Can't you just picture it, Peter? Shepherds piping their flocks home on purple hills and women with water jugs on their heads wending their way toward white stone cottages, and the lost Ulysses coming in over the wine-dark sea, his crew bursting into song. There must have been many Ulysseses, many Penelopes to welcome the wanderers home from the sea.

"Peter, these people are like that. I couldn't speak their language, but it was as though I had known them for

143

all the years of my life. When you make friends you can't desert them, Peter."

"You're strong enough to write out your report," I said. "Perhaps you'd better get started."

He shook his head stubbornly. Then his lips tightened and he looked at me steadily for an instant and spoke with a pleading urgency. "Peter, you can't even begin to understand how beautiful their culture is. To see it disappear—"

It was a new experience for me, walking along a silent corridor with just a little square medical case and the clothes on my back. You can't teleport a laboratory to the stars, and a physician without all the equipment he's likely to need is at a great practical disadvantage.

At my side walked Ulno Drook. I was asking for it with a vengeance, but I did need a telepath and Drook had put up a very convincing argument. I'd be along to look after him, wouldn't I?

For the first time in my life I was stepping out of character and betraying a trust. When you take your life oath you give your promise to use your authority with calm maturity.

The walk to the stars was tremendous, but a physician had no right to take it.

Approaching the teleport I could hear Seaton saying: "When you make friends it's hard to desert them, Peter lad."

He knew I was a pushover for that kind of talk. I had a healthy respect for explorers who refused to become bleeding hearts, but I did happen to be a physician. You take your oath and you can't quite forget that your job is to heal.

The teleport seemed to wink at us in chill mockery.

"Wait three minutes before you step in after me, Drook," I said.

"I'll be careful, Peter."

I squared my shoulders and braced myself against the terrible hammer-blow to the solar plexus which the scanners delivered before they blacked you out.

Then— I stepped forward into a roaring sea of light . . .

The houses were beautiful beyond belief. Thirty or forty one-storey houses, shining crystal bright in garish sunlight, each dwelling surrounded by thickets, and winding rustic paths and gardens bright with blue and vermilion flowers.

The teleport lay behind us on a russet hillside, its entrance choked with creeping vines. I'd emerged by pushing the vines aside and crawling out with scant regard for my dignity. Drook had scrambled out after me, and we'd descended the hill together.

There didn't seem to be any people about.

I turned to Drook and asked him if he could pick up any human thoughts.

He shook his head. "Not a thing, Peter!"

"The village can't be deserted," I protested. "Seaton left less than three hours ago."

"It doesn't take long to abandon a village," Drook said.

I vaguely sensed that he was disturbed, and I couldn't help noticing that the scene before us seemed to lay a spell on him, heightening his gnomish aspect and diminishing his talkativeness. I found it necessary to remind myself that the qualities which made an explorer great couldn't be learned in schoolrooms.

Drook knew how to adjust quickly to the baffling aspects of a new world, to blend with its strangeness and beauty chameleon fashion until it yielded up its inmost secrets.

145

"The houses are transparent, Peter," he said. "If we were closer we could look inside and see the people."

"But you just said—"

"You asked me if I could pick up any random thoughts, Peter." Drook's voice was calm and precise. "There are people in all of the houses, but they are either asleep or dead; sometimes it's hard to tell."

People in all of the houses.

People asleep or dead.

The village was less than three hundred feet away, and I headed toward it on the run. Drook's words had come as a shock and filled me with an ominous foreboding. But what I saw as the individual dwellings ceased to glimmer and became blocks of completely transparent crystal was so startlingly beautiful that I experienced for an instant no sense of tragedy.

Then it hit me.

Clad in white and flowing robes which seemed to blend with their graceful limbs they sat about like exquisitely beautiful statues in a museum. We went from house to house and what we saw filled us with a pity so great we could only stare and shake our heads.

The people were not dead. I took their pulses, and their hearts were beating steadily. But they had all fallen into a deep sleep, the sleep of utter exhaustion.

In one house there was a baby sitting upright in a wooden cradle. He was gripping a wooden spoon and making faces in his sleep. Shaking failed to rouse him.

There was a woman so beautiful she brought a catch to my throat. There was an old man who looked like Socrates slumped above a butter churn, his long beard descending to his chest. There was a pair of young lovers, holding hands.

Apparently they had gone to sleep starry-eyed together.

Each house was furnished with great simplicity and beauty. There were three-legged chairs and tables carved of some dark resinous wood that filled the rooms with a forest fragrance, and brightly coloured urns and vases decorated with lines of strange flying birds resembling wild geese in wedge-shaped formations.

There were rude spinning wheels, polished to a shining brightness, and wooden cradles on rockers, their sides decorated with carvings of scenes from daily life which showed an amazingly bold and free quality of imagination.

I was standing in a large bright room staring at a sleeping child when I heard the footsteps. They were coming up the path outside, and they were slow and lagging, as if a man worn out with weariness was having great difficulty in placing one foot before the other.

Drook stiffened and gripped my arm. "It's the father of that kid," he said, gesturing toward the cradle. "I can read his thoughts clearly. He's worn out with pain and grief, and he's been searching for his wife all afternoon. His wife went into the forest to look for—"

Drook hesitated. "Something very strange, Peter. His wife went into the forest to search for a giant."

"A giant?"

"*The* giant. There's only one, apparently. There is great torment and uncertainty in his mind. He's unable to understand why the giant has not come to relieve his weariness. He is cold and frightened, and he has a stone dagger."

Drook stiffened in sudden alarm. "Careful, Peter. He's at the door!"

The footsteps became very loud suddenly, and we both froze.

The man who stood framed in the doorway was a little above medium height, with a lean handsome face and tousled dark hair. Torment and shock looked out of his eyes, and his hands shook and he stood staring at us in silence for a moment. First at Drook in stark disbelief, and then at me.

I saw suspicion and then unmistakable hostility flare in his eyes. That didn't surprise me. I was a stranger, and all strangers were to be feared by a people just emerging from barbarism in a world of Homeric marauders wading in from the sea, plundering and singing as they came.

He might have been less frightened if I hadn't been accompanied by a gnome. Whether there were gnomes in his mythology I had no way of knowing, but a man who believed in giants could hardly fail to be chilled by a Martian.

I saw him draw the knife, but I stood my ground. His movements were pitifully slow and fumbling, and I was sure I could handle him if he took it into his head to lunge at me. Something caught at the corner of my eye, and I saw that Drook was edging away from him, and gesturing to me to do likewise.

I must have been quite mad. He came at me with a hoarse groan, and before I could leap back the knife was at my throat.

I had never been quite so close to death. With one hand he gripped my shoulder, and with the other held the knife pressed to my jugular.

You poor, poor devil, I thought. He was going to kill me, but it would have done me no good to hate him. We

148

were separated by gulfs of space and time and language; he had been made desperate by the ebbing of his strength, and the need to protect his home from a marauder bent on pillage. I had failed to realize how quickly a desperate fear could iron out the kinks in the muscles of an exhausted man.

Quite suddenly he collapsed. The knife clattered to the floor, and he sank down and started crying like a crazy man. He dragged himself away from me across the floor to the cradle. With a great effort he lifted himself up, and looked down at his kid.

He reached out a hand, and rubbed the knuckles gently over the sleeping youngster's face. Then he sank down again with a rasping sob of sheer exhaustion. I watched his breathing become shallow and almost stop.

The first thing a good physician does when he's faced with a problem of exhaustion is have a look at the patient's blood. With Drook assisting I got my medicine case open, and a neat little portable hematokrit set up.

Now with an ordinary two capillary tube hematokrit a blood count is quite simple. The tubes are attached to a centrifuge, and when the specimen is whirled about the number of red cells is estimated from the scale on each tube.

Unfortunately nature is a consistent wench only to a degree. Parallel evolution gives you humans more often than it gives you gnomes like Drook on the planets of ten thousand suns.

But you don't always get the kind of blood you can whirl in a centrifuge and measure on a capillary tube scale. Or the kind you can analyse further by staining, and a specific gravity test.

This time we were in luck.

What we got was the kind of blood that ran red in my own veins. Only—it wasn't red. It was faded, down to a few thousand red cells a cubic millimeter. Brother, that's low.

It was the most frightening reduction in erythrocytes I'd ever seen, and indicated a nutritional deficiency state so grave that the sleeping men and women had no right to be alive.

I looked at Drook. The man by the table was still breathing, but his eyes were shut, and he had long since ceased to mutter to himself.

We were working by a table which was in the same style of art as the chairs and tables. There was a design cut in the wood which had puzzled and disturbed me before I'd set up the hematokrit. Now it took on ominous implications.

It showed a dozen small human figures with their arms extended in pitiful appeal. Their legs had given way and they were reaching up beseechingly toward a gigantic pair of hands which hovered in the air directly above them.

"It begins to make sense," I said. "The pieces are falling into place."

"I'm glad they're not dreaming, Peter," Drook said. "I'm glad they're sleeping the deep, dreamless sleep of exhaustion."

His eyes filmed with imagined pain. "I doubt if I could endure the despair which would come to them in dreams, I'd have to get out fast."

"They were reduced to despair by famine," I said. "Poor harvests, the dying of their livestock. It's the old, tragic story. The land isn't quite fertile enough. Advanced agriculture could save them, but their husbandry is too crude to turn the trick."

I tapped the hematokrit. "Their diet must have been badly deficient in essential proteins and amino acids. When that occurs over a long period, the body loses its natural ability to synthesize factors necessary for blood building."

· "Is there no way to help them?" Drook asked.

"We could teach them scientific agriculture," I said. "But it would take months. From childhood they've been taught to believe that they can solve all of their problems by appealing to the giant; I only wish it was as simple as that."

"The giant?"

"A forest giant," I said. "It's an almost universal human myth. The giant is a symbol of agricultural fertility. A mythical deity who goes striding across an impoverished land scattering golden grain in rich abundance."

"Can nothing be done for them, Peter?"

"They'll need stiff shots of concentrated nutrients," I said: "we'll have to go back to the station for the ampoules. But before we cross the bridge I'm going to have a closer look at the land itself.

"The village is hemmed in by a forest, but there must be open farm country within easy walking distance. These people don't live by hunting and fishing; their art shows unmistakably that they're in the settled agricultural stage."

"I don't know, Peter," Drook said, about twenty minutes later by the watch on his beanstalk wrist, a watch that had crossed light millennia without ceasing to keep perfect time. "You may be right, of course; but this forest seems to be endless." ·

· He stopped to mop his wrinkled grey brow and stare up at a little patch of faded blue sky.

"We'll find tilled fields if we keep on," I said. "These people had to get their food from the land."

"I wonder," said Drook.

I was losing patience with him, but he was so infernally sensitive I didn't want to come right out and upbraid him.

I saw him wince as he tuned in on my thoughts.

"You're not an explorer, Peter," he said. "I am. I say that with the utmost humility. When you've been to the stars fifty or sixty times you can get the feel of a forest like this. Just by instinct, Peter. You can put your ear to the ground without actually seeming to do so."

"All right," I said. "Suppose you tell me what's up ahead. Say—a mile ahead."

"Something that frightens me," Drook said quickly. "It's breathing like an animal in pain. There are no thoughts in its mind, but there's a kind of crying, you know how a frightened child whimpers and cries in the dark."

I looked at him for a long moment in silence. "Well— we'll soon know! " I said.

I wasn't quite sure whether I believed Drook or not. But if his purpose had been to unnerve me, he'd certainly succeeded. When I saw the light of the clearing gleaming between the trees confidence was at a low ebb, and I didn't much feel like pressing on.

But press on I did. I was determined to settle it once and for all, and I stepped out from between the trees with one thought uppermost in my mind. Drook was all right. A better companion had never accompanied a man to the stars. But I couldn't have him unnerving me by sending his mind leaping ahead and conjuring up imaginary dangers. I couldn't—

The forest seemed to shake and sway about me. I

152

caught my breath and for the first time in my life that I could remember I knew stark, unreasoning fear.

The giant lay sprawled out in the clearing with his knees drawn up, his arms flung wide. Golden leaves spilled over him, and a swarm of iridescent insects formed a cloud about his head.

He was at least fourteen feet tall, and his fat fleshy pink body was clothed in a shining garment which glistened with dew. His eyes were closed and his chest rose and fell with his breathing and there was a great jagged gash on his forehead which was invisible from a distance of fifty feet.

I don't know how long I might have stood there staring if Drook hadn't moved quickly past me. There was no fear in him, and his courage made me realize I was behaving like a fool.

The giant had been knocked cold by a falling tree. The tree lay across his chest, pinning him to the ground, and his face was twisted in pain.

It wasn't the face of a grown man; it was the face of a child. The forehead bulged and there were little dimples in the pink and white cheeks. It was the face of a child of seven or eight but it was grotesquely mature in some respects, puckered and chillingly wise.

"He's been knocked out cold," Drook said.

I nodded, looking at the strange, glittering object in the child giant's hand.

It didn't look like a hypodermic, exactly; it was shaped differently, and there were two needles instead of one, and the plunger was a solid metal job.

But it was a hypodermic, all right.

I knelt and took the child giant's pulse. His heart was

153

beating slowly but steadily. I noticed that his skin was pale and clammy and felt cold to the touch.

"He's in a stupor," I said. "The tree knocked him unconscious, all right, but just how long he's been lying here is anybody's guess. I've a feeling it may have been several days."

"What does it mean, Peter?" Drook asked, his voice hardly audible.

"Something very strange," I said. "If I'm guessing right —it doesn't do violence to any natural law. But it presupposes the existence of an intelligence that isn't native to this planet."

"What kind of intelligence, Peter?"

"That can wait," I said. "Remember what I said about the forest giant? A myth hasn't warm blood in its veins, and a myth can't be knocked unconscious by a falling tree; so the forest-giant goes out the window."

On an impulse I lowered my hand until my palm rested on the child giant's cold right arm. "He's not what I thought he was," I said. "But he's needed here as no myth could ever be needed. Without him, the people perish; he's as much a part of them as they are of him."

Drook said: "What are you going to do, Peter?"

"Revive him," I said.

"Revive him, Peter. How?"

"A quick-acting stimulant to the heart, brain, muscles and spinal cord should wake him up," I said. "I'll try a shot of caffeine; it's safer than a few other drugs I could use."

With Drook hovering at my elbow I knelt, opened the little black case again, and took out what I needed.

I gave the giant a shot in the right arm.

We didn't stay very close to him. Drook retreated further than I did, taking refuge behind a big rotting tree trunk at the edge of the clearing. He looked more than ever like a gnome crouching there in shadows, his big ears alert to every sound.

Watching a sleeping giant wake up can be a nerve-shattering experience. When you're responsible it can give you an ill-defined sense of guilt which isn't an easy thing to rationalize.

He woke up slowly. First his eyelids twitched and then one of his limbs jerked spasmodically. His breathing became louder, his chest rose and fell, and he made a gulping sound.

Then, abruptly, he sat up.

He sat up and stared around him, and his face was the face of a child awakening in a dark room, and blinking in a sudden burst of light from an opening door.

He looked frightened, then puzzled, then reassured. He staggered to his feet and raised his hand and stared down at the strange looking hypodermic. Then his mouth began to work and I thought for a moment he was going to cry. I thought he was going to break down and blubber.

Instead, his infant laughter rang out suddenly in the still forest, clear and joyous and carefree. Not infant laughter exactly—childish laughter. Before its echoes could die away, he'd turned and was crashing through the under-brush like a seven-year-old interrupted in his play who must hurry to make up for all the fun he's missed.

But it wasn't fun he'd missed, and when we caught up with him in the village fifteen minutes later he was no longer laughing. He was kneeling before one of the houses, and lifting the exhausted men and women out through an open window into the sunlight.

He was setting them down and injecting them one by one. There was a tender concern in his face, and more wisdom than I had ever thought to see in the eyes of a child.

We stood in shadows, Drook and I, and watched him.

"I don't know exactly what's in that syringe, but I can make a pretty good guess," I said. "Tracer minerals, and just the right nucleic acid hydrolysis and aerobic fermentation products. He'll overcome their nutritional deficiency so fast you'll be able to see the colour creep back into their cheeks."

That was a slight overstatement of course. Actually it would take three or four days. But in a few days—and when I shut my eyes I could see it—the village would come back to life. There would be laughter in the houses again. Strange moons would rise and set, and infants with chubby cheeks would sit up in their cradles, and women with golden hair would smile warmly down at them.

They would never have to worry about wresting a living from the land. Even the men would not have to work in the fields, but would be free to create objects of beauty all day long. No wonder the village craftsmanship was so superb.

"They will never know," I said. "There will never be any need for them to know."

"You say he came from another part of space?" Drook whispered. "A child of some tremendous super race? What makes you so sure, Peter?"

"It is all of a piece," I said. "At most, our teleports span a hundred thousand light years. We have just barely reached to the far edge of the Galaxy. There are giant suns beyond for a million times that distance, from the Whirl-pool Nebula to the farthest intergalactic gap within range of our telescopes."

"But he is a human child."

"Where in space has man not encountered his own face mirrored large," I said.

"Then we are no longer needed here, Peter."

"You'll be glad to get back to your painting," I said, consolingly. "And now that you're certified as healed, you won't have to stay at the Station. You can go out again tomorrow, if you wish."

"With you, Peter?"

"I'm not an explorer," I said.

Drook straightened, his eyes shining, the gnome-face half in brightness. "And you'll be glad to see Seaton again, and talk this over with him, and tell him what you've accomplished."

"How did you guess it," I said.

"Peter, if we moved out from these bushes and let him see us—"

"Are you out of your mind?" I snapped. "What would we gain by that? Would you have him mistake me for a villager?"

"Just to see the expression on his face, Peter."

"No," I said, very firmly. "It's time we started moving. I'll grant you that. But—"

"A child has to learn and grow," Drook said, musingly. "And good parents believe in independence, too. Send a child away to school; give him a whole planet for a play-ground and workshop."

"That's about it," I said.

He nodded. "All right, Peter; let's go."

We didn't attempt to cross through the village to the field beyond. We circled the village through a woody patch, and approached the teleport at a leisurely walk, as if we had all the time in the world.

Drook asked me one more question before we scraped away the vines. "They wouldn't have to be mechanical in a strict sense."

"Not at all," I said.

We went back to Earth across tens of thousands of light years, firm friends one moment, the next a swirl of anti-gravitics in the gulfs between the stars.

Drook emerged thinking of bright pigments on canvas, and the loneliness of the ward and how good it would be to go out to the stars again. At least, that was my guess.

I emerged thinking of my darling. I told myself I'd go right up to Ward H, and punch my off-duty card, and we'd dine in that smoky little restaurant even if it meant I'd fall asleep at the table and dream about giants. Jack the Giant Killer or maybe the Cyclops who terrorized Ulysses and his crew on a high cliff above the wine-dark sea. There were some pretty formidable giants in our mythology, too.

But I had guessed wrong about Drook. He wasn't wondering if he really had what it took to go Gauguin one better. He was still thinking about the beautiful village we'd left dreaming in the light of an alien sun.

"A child sent away to school," he murmured, close at my heels. "Given a whole planet for a playground and workshop. The modern tendency is to make them as life-like as possible. A child learns more quickly that way. His sympathies are more directly appealed to."

Giants there were in those days. A quotation ... Biblical.

158

Giants in the earth. In a minute, I told myself, we'd be at the door of Ward C. I'd stop walking abruptly, and Drook would take his departure with a steady handclasp, and a shake of the gnome-head. He'd drift off into the ward.

"Peter, those villagers knews about the giant. But they wouldn't have to know; they could just—run down. Then the giant would restore them, and they'd go right on where they left off. If the giant were really clever, he'd never let them know. He'd never show himself at all. He might have to at first, but later on he'd keep out of sight."

I turned and faced him. "All right, say it," I demanded; "get it off your chest."

"He'd never let them know, Peter, that they were merely ingenious educational toys."

THE END

www.ingramcontent.com/pod-product-compliance
Lightning Source LLC
Chambersburg PA
CBHW020647180626
46816CB00003B/1166